HIKE AND
THE AEROPLANE

HIKE AND THE AEROPLANE

SINCLAIR LEWIS
Writing as Paul Graham

WILDSIDE PRESS

**TO
EDWIN AND ISABEL LEWIS, THE
AUTHOR'S OLDEST FRIENDS**

**Originally published in 1912.
wildsidepress.com**

CHAPTER I

A RESCUE IN CANYON DIABLO

TWO boys were riding on horseback along a little trail that overhung Canyon Diablo. They were exploring the lonely country miles below Monterey, on the California coast. Above them rose the mountains; a thousand feet below them was the Diablo River. The boys were dressed in khaki, with puttees, and with broad-brimmed felt hats that looked as though they had slept in them and used them for dippers and footballs.

The strong United States cavalry horses which they rode seemed to be ready for anything, and the boys themselves did not act as though they were much afraid of a drop from this narrow shelf of rock.

Hike Griffin, who rode ahead, was a boy of sixteen, with straight shoulders that were going to become very broad. He had a shock of the blackest hair that ever grew, and quiet, gray eyes that never seemed to worry. His mouth was strong, yet with little laughter-wrinkles at the side, as though he saw life as an interesting joke.

He rode so easily that he almost slouched in his saddle, like a cow-puncher. But when the horse reared at a rabbit that started up from the chaparral, he straightened up like a cavalry officer leading a squadron on parade, and coaxed her into behaving, laughing at her and patting her neck.

That was just the way Hike Griffin had handled the Freshman football team at Santa Benicia Military Academy, all the fall before. "Hike" wasn't his only name. His father, Major James Griffin, of the army Signal Corps, had named him Gerald. Hike had feared that the fellows at Santa Benicia would call him "Geerawld."

They started to, but when he took his hazing like a man, and captured the hearts of all his classmates, he was christened "Jerry." Then he became right half and captain of the Freshman football team. With a splendid sixty-yard run or "hike" as westerners call it, he made the touch-down which won the Freshmen's great annual game with San Dinero Prep.

While he was dashing down the field with the ball under his arm, the Santa Benicia rooters went mad, yelling "Hike, Jerry, hike! Griffin, hike, *hike*!" After that, he was known as "Hike." The same meaning, said Poodle Darby, "to go with speed, like a whale-fish!"

In the spring, he had done some more hiking, when he won the half-mile and cross-country races, running along easily, as though he were a little chilly, and wanted to get warm. There was no more danger that he would be insulted by "Geerawld."

So he was quite happy when he went home to the Monterey Presidio for summer vacation, and took with him his classmate and roommate, Torrington Darby.

You must not think that Torrington Darby was *called* that! You would have known he couldn't have been, if you had seen him—round, sleek as a dove, always grinning all over his happy face, and usually drawling songs he made up himself; very lazy and very cheerful. Just the same he always got his lessons. In fact, he was much quicker at the books than was Hike.

He made life so interesting to all his friends that they decided he must have a better handle than "Torrington." So they sat upon him, one evening; one on his face and another on his chest, while a third tied up his legs. This was so that he could not interfere with their important decision. Darby looked very patient and folded his hands and whined like a small dog, after kicking Left Eared Dongan vigorously; so they named him "Poodle," and made him beg for small sticks, out in the Yard.

It was Poodle Darby who was riding behind Hike Griffin, along the canyon trail, making the day hideous by singing that good California chant, "Hallelujah, I'm a bum."

They had been out on the trip for four days, and the excellent Poodle had sung that thing ninety thousand, seven hundred and steen times, Hike figured.

"Come on, Poodle; we'll have to hustle if we're going to reach the top of the trail for camp to-night," Hike shouted.

> "Oh, why don't you work, as other men do—
> All right then, hike, Hike, and I'll fol-lol-low you!"

So Poodle carelessly bawled back, and ground his heel into the side of his horse, kicking it into a canter.

The horse started. A rock slipped on the hillside above and rattled down, striking her flank. She flung up her head. Poodle vainly pulled on the rein, as she pranced skittishly.

Her back feet slipped. Over the side of the trail she slid. She pawed furiously with her front hoofs, but could not get hold of the slippery rock. She was surely sinking—close to the drop of a thousand feet.

For a moment her rear hoofs stuck, safe, on a tiny ledge.

Poodle cried "Hike!" once. Then he was silent, trying to keep from thinking of the awful drop below him.

Hike looked around. He did not make a sound. He spurred his horse, reached a broader spot in the trail, turned, and came loping back.

Quietly he said to Poodle, "Jump."

"Can't—make her lose footing," stammered Poodle.

Hike dropped from his horse and ventured down the side of the cliff. His calmness gave courage to the trembling Poodle. He held out his hand and commanded, "Put foot on that. Jump."

Poodle obeyed. Hike clutched an old mesquite root with his left hand, to hold himself in place, and almost threw Poodle up to safety. The horse was not dislodged from the position to which she desperately clung.

Taking her bridle, Hike coaxed. She shivered, but would not move. As quietly as though he were petting her in the stable, Hike rubbed her nose and urged her. Still she would not move.

"Got to hoist her up." Hike bit off his words as though he were running a team-play. "Here, Pood', fasten bridle to my saddle-horn. Hustle. I'll make my horse drag her up. Say, if both horses get pulled off trail, I'll jump. Try catch me."

"Oh, don't try it!" Poodle's round face was very serious.

"Fasten that BRIDLE, I said!" ordered Hike. His voice sounded like his father's, on the parade ground.

Poodle jumped to obey. Hike got on his own mount, still soothing the horse that was in danger. Resolutely turning his back, Hike touched the rowel to his nag.

With the bridle tugging sharply at her, Poodle's horse started, scrambled frantically at the edge of the cliff, climbed, wavered, then bolted up, with heaving back, safe on the trail.

Poodle sat down, looking very pale, now that the danger was over. He grinned at Hike, who had dismounted and was patting the shivering, excited horses. It was a very sick young grin, but Poodle worked over it for a while, and it got much better. He drawled:

"Say, Hike, that was fine scenery from that ledge."

"Um," said Hike, after thinking it over.

"You're dead right," agreed Poodle. "That's what I was thinking. Don't look so blooming serious about it, though."

"Well, you'd look serious if you had to spend all your time when you weren't sleeping rescuing Poodles from death," remarked Hike.

"I do!" stated Poodle. "Say, I thought I was going to be an aeroplane there, for a second. No, I thought my horse was goin' to be! But gee! I was wondering how I could deflect her front—"

"Nice word, deflect."

"—control when we struck the canyon down there.... Maybe the joke'd have been kinda *flat*, like me, if it hadn't been for you, Hike. Much obliged for rescuing me. I oughtn't to get killed to-day, 'cause I promised to write Mother about the scenery down the coast."

"So thoughtful of you," said Hike. "You're a good young un, Pood'. I got twice as scared as you."

"Sure. That was why my teeth was chattering so. I was so scared you'd get scareder. Le's hike."

"Right," remarked Hike, and they mounted and rode on. They were pretty quiet for a mile, and there were no races. At the end of it, Poodle called:

"Hike."

"Uh-huh."

"Say—I was awful scared."

"So was I," Hike grinned back, and they both laughed.

Before dusk, they reached the peak at the head of the canyon, and looked down on the other side of the San Francisquito range of mountains. A hundred little valleys stretched in all directions. There were no signs of human life. Many of these valleys had never been visited by any white man except some wandering prospector looking for gold mines. One of the ravines led to a valley at least a mile wide, flat and grassy, with a comfortable brook flowing through it.

"Gee, that's a great country down there," observed Poodle. "We'll explore it. Jiminy, this is *great*—feels like we were the first white men in America." Tethering his horse, he stood on the edge of an arroyo leading down from the peak.

"What d'you say to the first white men getting some wood before it's too dark?" murmured Hike, rooting out a big log.

"If you weren't a nice young man, I'd think that was a hint," retorted Poodle, quite cheerfully. "If I catch the idee, you b'lieve we might use a little fire-wood."

"No, that ain't it at all. I just thought we might need some toothpicks after dinner. 'Course we'll do the cooking in some moonlight," explained Hike. "Nice hot moonlight."

"Well, now, I'd almost suppose you were gettin' sarcastic," said Poodle, "but 'course if you don't *want* me to help you ketchum heap plenty wood, why, I'll have a small game of mumble-te-peg." He opened his knife, but, as he started his game, one Hike, a person of much muscle, picked him up, carried him over to the remains of a dead fir tree, and murmured, "Want to get dropped down the arroyo?"

"A hint's always enough for little Poodle," declared that cheerful gentleman, and got busy with twigs and branches.

When dusk came, they were frying bacon stuck on sharpened twigs, and singing "Hallelujah, I'm a bum." Coffee was singing with them, in the pot among the coals. Poodle stated that he could eat a whole grocery store, including the scales, wrapping paper, and cashier. (He didn't have the chance to prove whether he could or not, however, for even so husky a boy as Hike doesn't usually carry a whole grocery store at the cantle of his saddle when he goes on a riding trip.)

With the bacon and flapjacks and syrup and coffee inside them, the two boys lay with their feet to the fire. They had forgotten the strain of the rescue on the cliff-side. They were just sinking off into sleep, looking so comfortably and dreamily at the cheerful fire, when Poodle started up, awakened by the sound of a coyote's howl nearby.

"Say, I thought I heard something besides a coyote," he said. "Sounded like hammering—and there ain't a human within twenty miles of us. Even if there was a smuggler on the coast, he'd be five miles away."

"Yes," replied Hike, very quietly, "I've been listening to it for five minutes. It *is* a man hammering—on iron—and there can't be anybody down in those valleys—and there *is*!... Well, we'll find out in the morning. Some mystery, some mys—some—" Hike was asleep.

"Should say there *was* a mystery," grunted Poodle, sticking just the tip of his button of a nose from the top of his blanket. "Think you might get a little bit scared, anyway. You oughta be. It's a mys— It sure is— I dunno—"

Alas, we can never know what Poodle didn't know, for by this time the only thing awake around that camp on the peak was a lone coyote, who came over and reflectively ate the top of one of Poodle's shoes. And still the mysterious hammering kept up, down in the wilderness of valleys.

CHAPTER II

THE MYSTERY OF THE HAMMERING

"DON'T stop and make too many poems about the valleys, Poodle," commanded Hike Griffin, after breakfast.

"Star of the gridiron, I ain't making po'ms. I'm beating the job and getting in a loaf on you," Poodle Darby assured him, as, with chin in hand, he looked across the wonderful green hills stretched far below the peak where they had camped all night. "Say, I've been listening for that duffer that was pounding iron so late, and I thought I heard him, over there to the sou'-sou'-east."

"You've got a great little ole brain, Pood'. You hit it right. Us for the mystery of the hammering. Probably a stray bunch of cattlemen, riding the ranges. Probably shoeing their horses. Peaceful as pie."

"Yuh," grinned Poodle. "Think it's counterfeiters?"

"Yes. 'S matter of fact, I do." Hike was very quiet about it, but Poodle looked up admiringly. The young captain of the Freshman football team acted as though he meant very busy business.

Leaving their horses tethered, and their food cached, except for a little bacon, tea, and rice, they scrambled down an arroyo, crawled down a rockface, with fingers and toes clinging to ledges, and reached a long slope covered with thick chaparral, through which Hike forced a way, with Poodle cheerfully trotting after him. They reached the beginning of the mile-broad valley which they had noticed the night before. A small hill separated it from them. As they started to mount this hill, on the other side of it sounded a clatter and banging, as though a giant blacksmith shop were in operation.

"Hssshhhh!" came from Hike, as Poodle started to exclaim. Up the hill swung Hike, his shoulders low, making himself as small as he could, but with his long slender legs going like propeller-blades on a motor boat. At the top Hike crouched down; then held up his hands and said—still peering across the crest—"Well, I'll be everlastingly hornswoggled."

Poodle always had to talk about something. Though he was wild with desire to see what there was on the other side, he stopped, shook his chubby forefinger at Hike, and said in the tones of the headmaster at Santa Benicia Academy, "Griffin, this is shocking. What words! What wick-ed, lit-tle wor-dies!"

"Choke yourself to death and come here," retorted Hike, and Poodle crawled up beside him. He saw, in a grassy hollow opening on the broad valley, a long, high, wide shed, like a cow stable ten times enlarged. Beside it was a forge with a pile of metal—pistons and bolts and motor-wheels; and spread out on the grass was something like a big box-kite slightly twisted. Not a person was in sight.

"Well, I'll be completely swigbottled!" stated Poodle. "Say, Hike, what is it all? D'you know?"

"Torr*ing*tum, this is very sad. Such wick-ed words from the mouth of—"

"Oh, *shut* up. What is it? I'll foam at the mouth in about—"

"It's an aerodrome, I'd say—shed for an aeroplane. Too small for a dirigible balloon. And that box-kite thing there by the forge looks to me like part of some daffy sort of a plane. Poodski, I reckon we've run into some crazy aviator's shop.... Counterfeiter nothin'!"

"Well, if that gent thinks *that* thing is an aeroplane wing, he's counterfeiting aeroplanes, anyway," complained Poodle. "I never *saw* such a ridiculousness."

"Come on," said Hike—a remark which he made very often, or so said Poodle, who now complained, "Every time I get settled down and comfy, looking at nice valleys, or an asylum for nutty aviators, you go and drag me away. Well, lead on, gallant captain."

As they descended the slope, out of the shed, keeping his back toward them, came the strangest man they had ever seen. He was dressed in one single garment of white—"a night-shirt that's crazy as he is," sniffed Poodle—with leather sandals on his feet, and with his wild, black hair falling to his shoulders. As he turned, they both cried out with wonder. The man's black beard reached his chest. Even twenty feet away, they could see his eyes shining like a wild animal's among the knotted hair that was towsled over his forehead. In his hand was a rod of metal. As he saw them he shrieked and started back, then rushed at them, waving the iron rod, and shouting "Go away! For your lives. G' 'way!"

He came up to them, stopped, and bellowed, "You boys get out of this or I'll kill you. I'll give you till I get my rifle, and if you ain't gone then— I'll brain you—I'll kill you—"

He came nearer, still waving the iron rod. There was quick team-play. Hike and Poodle picked up sticks, without a word. They separated and came at the man from opposite sides. He stopped. He dropped the iron rod. He ran his fingers through his beard and shouted, "What do you want? Whom are you spying for?"

"No one," explained Hike. "We've just been on a riding trip—down the coast from Monterey. Rode up Canyon Diablo, and came down this side of the Big Peak. Didn't know there was anybody here. I'm awf'ly interested in aeroplanes, though. You see, my father—Major Griffin—I'm Jerry Griffin, this is Torry Darby—he's in command of the Signal Corps at Monterey Presidio. Honest, I don't want to butt in, but that funny box-kite thing there made me awf'ly interested. If we're intruding, we'll beat it, but I'd like to learn something about that thing.... You see I've been reading a bunch about aeroplanes, and Lieutenant Adeler—Jack Adeler, you know, invented the Adeler hydroaeroplane, the one that beat the record rising from the water—well, he's at Monterey, and he's showed me a lot about aeroplanes...."

The man said nothing. He had seated himself upon a rock, twisting away at his long beard, looking as though he were in despair. Poodle and Hike stared at each other. Knowing nothing whatever about aeroplanes, Poodle could only remark, "Jiminy, never would expect to find a flyin' machine shed back in the hills, *would* you? Hope we ain't butting in. We'll keep our mouths shut. I guess we're both gentlemen—or gentlekids, anyway!"

"Yes," continued Hike, while the man still kept silent, seeming not to hear. "I'm really sorry we found your place, if you feel—"

The man suddenly broke in, "Yes, that's the way it goes—Signal Corps and government money, and hydroaeroplane, and here I am, with the greatest aeroplane in the world, and hardly a cent left to finish it. If I had the army behind me— Once I thought I would—I'd finish my machine—go flying across the hills—make the government back me."

"I'd be glad to introduce you to my father and Lieutenant Adeler—and, and Captain Welch, though you won't—he isn't so nice, quite—if you'd come up to the Monterey Presidio, some time," stammered Hike, feeling very shy before this man, who looked as though he had lost his last friend. "I'm sure they'd be glad to help you."

The man threw back his head, shook his fist at the sky ("which didn't seem to mind being shook at," Poodle noticed), and roared: "I'm sure they wouldn't. Pigs—scoundrels—thieves—impostors—all of them. If they aren't in a conspiracy against me, it's because I've kept 'em from knowing anything about me."

Hike's eyebrows lifted. Poodle was thinking that he had looked just that way when the captain of the San Dinero Freshman team had made fun of Santa Benicia, before the game.

"Sir," said Hike, "you are speaking of my father and my friends. They are gentlemen, and they love the army. The army needs good aeroplanes. If yours is good, they would even forgive your talking the way you have!"

The man glared and shook his beard. Then he saw Poodle's happy face, with a smile hiding in his eyes. Suddenly the man laughed:

"You're both of you amusing little cusses, and hanged if I don't believe you're right. I apologize. I've been living here alone—not seeing anybody except a Portygee ranchero, that brings me my grub and tools and aeronautical journals. I guess I've kind of lost my party manners. Young sir, I apologize. I'll be glad to come up to Monterey and meet the officers—and I'll be glad to show you my machine. Fact is, if somebody with money doesn't back me, I can't go on. I'm broke. But I have it done now—the aeroplane itself is all done. I've even flown it a little. But all I've got for engine is an old 1909 fifty horse-power Gnome, and I need two hundred and fifty horse-power."

"Two hundred and fifty!" shrieked Hike. "Why, nobody uses over seventy or so. They tried a hundred and fifty in the French army contest, but it was too much."

"The French didn't have my aeroplane. It's the first really practical tetrahedral that—"

"Ouch!" cried Poodle, as the hard word hit his ears.

"Tet-ra-hé-dral—it's made up of a number of little parts that look like paper wings. Each of them is made up of two triangles, the bottoms together. Like this."

With an old nail, he scratched on a rock this plan of one of the tiny "wings":

"Yump," he went on. "I've finally worked out the complete tetrahedral aeroplane, following some plans of Alexander Graham Bell—the man who invented the telephone. You see, boys, with all these little planes put together, the air can get hold of lots more surface than it can on the ordinary aeroplane. It doesn't make any difference which way the aeroplane is turned, there's always planes for the air to get under and hold the machine. An ordinary aeroplane is like the sides of a wooden box that honey comes in, and mine is like the honey itself, with all the hundreds of little walls of wax.

"But," he insisted, "with all these wings, the weight of the whole thing is much less than an ordinary aeroplane would have if it had as much supporting surface as my machine has.

"So the tetrahedral can carry an engine that's enough bigger than the ordinary aeroplane to make her go much faster than the ordinary one. She could stand an engine that would send her at two hundred miles an hour, and I could guarantee your officers that she'd be able to carry enough gasoline so that she could fly across the country without even a single stop for fuel. And she could make that trip in thirty-five hours, or less—scoot right along at a hundred miles an hour—two hundred at a pinch.

"Another thing is: with all these planes, turned every which way, she'd flutter down like a butterfly, instead of falling hard, if the engine stopped on you, or anything happened to the aviator. That's the kind of a machine I've got! Martin Priest is my name. I've been working away on aeroplanes for ten years, and *now I've got the best in the world*!"

Martin Priest was standing up, waving his arms, and yelling. Poodle whispered, "Gee, he's sure got something, all right! Maybe fits!"

But Hike was used to seeing officer aviators grow enthusiastic, and he replied, "Bite yourself dead" to Poodle, before he answered the other, "That sounds great, Mr. Priest. I'd like awfully to see your machine."

Martin Priest led the way to the door of the aerodrome. Inside was a structure like a huge blunt wedge, made up of hundreds of the small wings. It was like a crowd of white butterflies, or the swarming of big white bees.

While the boys stood gaping at this strange cluster, and the rudder and elevating planes, Martin Priest ramped up and down, explaining, throwing about long words that made Poodle jump. They didn't get much out of the explanation, but at the end of it Hike turned to Priest and said:

"I'm not as old as Methusaleh, and I guess there's still at least a couple of things about aviating that I haven't learned, but I can see that this machine would be mighty safe, and I should think it could carry all sorts of a load. Well, I'll just grab the United States Army—or Lieutenant Adeler, anyway, and make him help you. I'll put the Army behind you!"

Martin Priest laughed. "That's a pretty large order for an old man like you, isn't it?" he asked Hike.

"Uh huh," calmly remarked that worthy. "But I'm goin' to do it. We'll be back here—couple of days—with Lieutenant Adeler.... Come on, you young Poodle."

"Uh huh," said Poodle. "Sure, I'll come.... But I was so comfortable sitting here on this box!" Groaning, he bestirred his round cheerful self to follow Hike's easy lope up the hill, toward their camp.

CHAPTER III

LIEUTENANT ADELER AND WIBBELTY-WOBBELTY

MAJOR JAMES GRIFFIN, commander of the Army Signal Corps at the Monterey Presidio, did not know that the two boys who came riding up to the door of his office were bearing a great message. He didn't even know that the taller was the great Hike Griffin. He believed him to be merely Jerry Griffin, Son. Why, sometimes he even thought of him as *Gerald* Griffin! And, to him, Poodle was only "the son of my old friend Tom Darby." So he was not much impressed when the boys came scurrying in; excited, though they were tired and what Poodle called "feak and weeble around the knees," from their hard fast ride back up the coast.

"Well, boys," smiled the tall, slender, gentle Major, "did you have a good ride?"

Hike explained that they'd had a good ride, a very good ride. That they hadn't minded sleeping under single blankets, after all. And that they had found the greatest aeroplane in the world.

The Major listened smilingly to their description of Martin Priest and his tet-ra-hé-dral (Hike stumbled over the word, and had to take it in sections, as though it were a circus train!) "Well, well, strange," said the Major. "I'll see you at dinner, boys. Better run along now, and get a hot tub."

He turned back to the pile of papers on his desk. Poodle, by raising his eyebrows, asked silently of Hike, "What shall we do?" Just as silently, Hike replied, "Nothing!" by wriggling his shoulders.

They left the office, got that hot bath, and went to find Captain Willoughby Welch. Though they did not like the Captain, he was next in rank to the Major.

Poodle had nicknamed him "Wibbelty-Wobbelty." Other people called him "that mean officer." Captain Welch was a man who always seemed to be sneering—and usually was. No one liked him, yet his manners were beautiful, and his reputation as a Signal Corps expert so great, that Hike couldn't help looking up to him and admiring him at times—though he never thought, for one single minute, of *loving* him, as he did splendid Lieutenant Jack Adeler. Captain Welch had been a teacher of physics, of electricity and light and heat, at West Point. When men began trying out aviation, he made so many wonderful flights, and clever inventions—such as a means of fastening bracing cords to the struts or props of planes—that

15

he became famous. He first went over to France, and got one of the first aero pilot's licenses in the world.

The War Department had detailed him to look into the whole matter of the different sorts of aeroplanes, for a report to a "Board of Aviation," which was to meet in Washington, late in August of that summer, with Brigadier General Thorne of the Signal Corps at the head of it. This board was to recommend what they considered the best aeroplane—and Congress was going to spend nearly a million dollars in buying aeroplanes of that sort. Their recommendation would probably be largely founded on what Captain Welch reported. So Hike was anxious to have the Captain look very carefully into the matter of poor Martin Priest's aeroplane. But he felt very doubtful. For Captain Welch had already announced that he would report favorably on the Jolls aeroplane.

Hike didn't like Mr. P. J. Jolls, the owner of the Jolls aeroplane and friend to Captain Welch. Mr. P. J. Jolls was a plump person, with rolls of fat at the back of his neck, which stuck out over his collar like layers of sausage. He had a loud voice and, as Poodle said, "was allus a-actin' like he thought he owned the universe and was comin' 'round to collect rent from you for bein' on his old earth!" Mr. P. J. Jolls had never been up in an aeroplane, and he had never invented one single bolt or wire. But he was very clever at money-making. After collecting several millions by selling patent medicines, shaving-soap, and fake mine-stock, he had cornered the aeroplane-market. Nearly every model of American monoplane or biplane, with all patents, was now owned by him. He had hired inventors to combine the best things about all the different sorts of machines in one Jolls monoplane and one Jolls biplane.

Captain Welch had announced that the Jolls machines were the best in the world. Lieutenant Adeler declared that there were better ones—that Jolls was an old fake—and Hike loved him for saying so. But Welch said that for his part he was sure Mr. P. J. Jolls would be recognized by Congress as the greatest aviator in the world. He seemed to think that Mr. Jolls was also one of the most lovable men in the world; and to be glad that Mr. Jolls was going to get Congress's good round million dollars.

He even had Mr. Jolls as a guest at the Monterey Presidio, and took him to the Officers' Club. All the other officers found that they had important engagements away from the club, when they heard Mr. Jolls' loud thick voice. Even Major Griffin, the most polite of all men, disappeared.

While he was at the Presidio, Mr. P. J. Jolls had once patted Poodle Darby on the head, and called him a "fine boy." Ten minutes later, Hike Griffin found Poodle washing the head that had just been thus patted, with strong yellow soap, meanwhile seriously singing to himself:

16

"I hope a sea of soap suds rolls
Above the grave of P. J. Jolls.
He patted me upon the head,
And oh! the orful thing he said;
He'll soon, I hope, be nice—and—dead!"

Hike had then sat on his legs, like a Turk, and raising his long arms declared, "Poodski, never before did I know that you are the greatest poet in the world, but now I see that you are."

* * * *

When Hike and Poodle found Captain Willoughby-Wibbelty Welch, lover of the aeroplanes of P. J. Jolls, the good Captain was smoking a long thin cigar, sitting in a Chinese wicker chair on the porch of his quarters. He smiled that silky, sneaky, snakey, sneery smile of his (at least, that's what Poodle said his smile was, afterwards), and called out as they came up the walk, "Ah! Home again, boys?"

"No," whispered Poodle to Hike. "We're still at the South Pole fishing for bread-fruit-fish with a crow bar. Foolish question eleventy thousand and one."

"Well, how did the gallant heroes find the long trek?" smiled Captain Welch.

"Great," Hike gravely said. "Captain, way down the coast—in a canyon, where he wouldn't be disturbed at his experiments—there's an aviator chap with a—uh—a tet-ra-hé-dral aeroplane that's the fastest machine in the world, and that'd carry the most weight. He hasn't got the engine to fly her right, but I wish I could get you to come down and talk it over with him. I'd like to bet you'd find it was just the machine the War Department is looking for, for the army aeroplane."

"What makes you think it's the fastest machine in the world?" Captain Welch was still smiling, but he looked more patronizing than ever.

"Why, he explained it to me, Captain. And I saw it. And it strikes me as so awf'ly reasonable. I'm sure it's worth some looking into, anyway." Hike felt fussed. His argument did not sound convincing.

"Why, my *boy*, there isn't a crank aviator on earth that won't tell you the fool machine he's made out of barrel hoops and cheese cloth would fly if he only had the engine. He *knows* it will, and won't you please let him have the money and you'll get seventy per cent. He's always sure it would pay you to look into it. Why, my *boy*, one of the principal tasks of the Signal Corps is keeping cranks with wonderful inventions away. They'd use up all your time, if you'd let them. You just take my advice and don't listen to them."

The Captain stood up, yawned like a nice tabby cat, smoothed his neat little mustache, smiled, and started to go into the house.

"O Captain," called Hike, "won't you come down—fine ride—and just take a *look* at the—"

"Couldn't. Really. Haven't time. Must finish up my report for the Board of Aviation," the Captain said, very sweetly, but as though he considered the business finished.

"Wibbelty!" whispered Poodle.

"Wobbelty!" whispered Hike.

Their last chance was in Lieutenant Jack Adeler, the youngest officer in the Signal Corps at Monterey.

Jack Adeler was the son of a quiet old gentleman who had left him five hundred thousand dollars, a ranch in Mexico, and the kindliest disposition that a man ever had. He had graduated from Yale, then entered the army, and was devoting a great deal of his own private fortune to aviation. He had never made such showy flights as had Captain Welch, and he never advertised his knowledge of aviation as did the Captain, but Hike had the feeling that he really knew about ten times as much about it. He was solidly built and quick and quiet, and he liked to have Hike and Poodle with him, and never was tired of answering their questions.

When they found him—playing golf on the Post links—he listened to their tale of Martin Priest and the tetrahedral. He said that he too was a little afraid that Priest was a crank; but he promised to ride down the coast with the boys and look over the machine.

They started the next day.

When they reached the secret valley beyond Canyon Diablo, the crank aviator was sitting on a soap-box, waiting for them. He had cut his hair, in a rough way, and had changed his crazy-looking white gown for overalls, a blue flannel shirt, and a greasy sweater-jacket. Poodle's opinion was that he had changed himself from a crazy prophet into a tramp, a hobo mechanic; but both Hike and Lieutenant Adeler said that he looked like an Edison, with his broad forehead, slender hands, and bright eyes.

"Well, I wish I could find out all them things, like you high-brows," sighed Poodle. "I admit that I'm a mutt. I ain't even sure but what I'm a wutt. So I hope you'll let me go to sleep on that nice soft grass, and not yell 'Come on' too quick."

Martin Priest seemed to have waked up. He spoke quickly and hopefully —just as Hike did when he was interested. He showed them the machine, and told them of the small flights he had taken with his broken-down engine.

He explained a hundred devices. For instance, there was the speed changing gear. His aeroplane was the only one that ran on several speeds, like an automobile, so that the aviator could fly at different rates without having to cut down the feed of the engine with the hand-throttle, every second. But there was a hand-throttle, too. Then, there were double control wires, running from the levers to the rudder and the elevating planes, so that, if one wire broke (a thing that has caused many an aviator's death) another would take its place.

For starting the machine from the seat—without having to have some one whirl the propeller till the engine was going—there was an electrical motor, which was a sort of boy of all work. For, when it was through its work as a motor, it became a dynamo, and filled up storage-batteries which worked the big electrical search-light, for use when the machine was flying at night. It also ran a tiny electric stove, placed at the side of the freight-platform, and warmed electric heating-pads placed on the aviator's seat to keep him warm.

But most important of all was that this machine *really* had what aviators call "automatic stability"—that is, the power to right itself, and not go tumbling down, when it was tipped up by bad winds, such as a "retarded following breeze." Most aeroplanes have little planes called "ailerons," which swing up and help to balance the aeroplane when it tips. They are worked by the aviator, and if anything happens to him, or to them, very quick trouble follows. But with the tetrahedral's many little planes, facing every way, the machine caught the air and righted itself no matter which way it leaned.

To all of this, Lieutenant Adeler listened without saying much. Even Poodle listened with interest, though he did keep repeating that "horrid long name," over and over—tet-ra-hé-dral, tet-ra-hé-dral—as though he couldn't get to like it very much!

The lieutenant poked about in the aerodrome, took off his cap and stuck his head into what Poodle called "the tetooreelederlum's innards," and looked over some drawings and photographs that Martin Priest had made of the tetrahedral's flight. (He had been taking photographs even when he was hundreds of feet up in the air, by having the camera's lens uncover automatically).

Finally, Adeler nodded a couple of times and said, "Good machine. I'm not sure but that she'd be the fastest and best in the world!"

Then Martin Priest shook hands all 'round, shouted "God bless you," and threw himself on the ground, sobbing like a child that wants its mother.

Adeler stood quietly waiting. When Martin Priest had got control of himself, the Lieutenant said:

"Of course she'll have to have a test. If she makes good, I'll be glad to back you. I happen to have a good deal of money—inherited it from my father. I'll furnish the coin and all the help I can. I'd like to have an aero-drome built for you near Monterey. And I'll do all I can to get the govern-ment Board of Aviation—that'll decide on what machine the Army is to buy —look over your tetrahedral. The Board meets in Washington, in August. That is, I will if she shows up well when we test her—and I think she will."

"See here, Lieutenant," stammered Martin Priest, "I can patch this old Gnome—she's a good engine, all right, but she was smashed up in an acci-dent, and I've just been able to tinker with her. Never had new parts for her. But we can fly as far as Monterey with her, all right. You people have three horses? Well, you, Lieutenant, and one of the boys come with me in the aeroplane—it'll carry all three of us, and what of my stuff here I need to keep—say two thousand pounds—pretty good load, eh? especially over these hills, with all the air-flaws there are. You'll notice there's a regular freight platform, aft in the machine. The other boy can ride back, and there's a young ranchero that lives across the hills that'll be willing to go with him, riding one horse and leading the other. "When does the Army Board of Aviation meet, did you say? What? In one month? Well, I could have the tetrahedral ready to fly then, all right. But what about getting a two hundred and fifty horse-power engine?"

"There's a man down in San Diego that tried to build a monster triplane, and he got a great big two hundred and thirty horse-power Kulnoch engine for her—you know, one of these new ones, air-cooled, with revolving cylin-ders, peach of an engine," said Lieutenant Adeler. "His machine never would fly, and he wants to sell the engine. We can get that in time."

Adeler, though he talked very quietly, had gone into the thing as though it was the one thing he counted on. Hike was so glad that he pounded Poo-dle on the back till that comfortable youth grappled with him mightily.

"We'll make that test," continued the Lieutenant. "Hike, you and Poodle draw lots to see which goes with us.... By the way, Mr. Priest, there's just one thing we've got to take into account. The only proper way that we can get this machine before the Board of Aviation is to interest Captain Welch in it. He's to report to them. He's—uh—a little—"

"Mulish," supplied Poodle.

"He's a little obstinate," the Lieutenant went on explaining. "But if the tetrahedral works out as well as I think she will, he can't help seeing her ad-vantages. And so he'll have to make a favorable report to the Board."

The boys drew lots to see which should have the flight in the tetrahedral, and which should ride horseback up to Monterey. Poodle won the aeroplane trip. He led Hike aside, and murmured, "Say, old Hike, let's draw three times. The only fair way."

"Don't you want to try the tetrahedral?" asked Hike.

"'S matter of fact, I don't," confessed Poodle.

Hike was a good deal amazed to find Poodle apparently afraid of the trial. He was so anxious to go himself that he gladly accepted the offer to change places.

Quick at acting and good at thinking though Hike was, there were many times when he did not think so quickly as jolly Mr. Poodle. It wasn't till long afterward that it occurred to him that Poodle had never seemed really afraid of *anything*; and that the chances were that he had given up the flight to please his beloved chum.

While they were talking, Lieutenant Adeler had been saying to Martin Priest, "What have you named the tetrahedral?"

"I hadn't planned anything, yet. I suppose the general sort of aeroplane will be called the 'Priest Model.' I think we ought to name this particular one after young Griffin there. If it hadn't been for him, I'd never have had even a chance at a chance.... What was that you called him—nickname —'Hike' was it? Why not call it *'Hike the First'*?"

"Too likely to get his name and the tetrahedral's mixed up, I should say," considered Lieutenant Adeler.

"Well, 'Hustle' is pretty much like 'Hike.' How about *'Hustle the First'*?"

"Fine."

The boys were called over and informed of the tetrahedral's name—by which they usually called her, afterwards. Hike blushed a poppy-red when he was told that the name was really in honor of him.

"Hurray for Hike's *Hustle!*" shouted Poodle, and he dragged Hike and the grave Lieutenant after him in a dance about the *Hustle*, singing:

> "Hallelujah, I'm a bum, hallelujah, bum again,
> Hurray-yay-yay for old Hike's aeroplane!"

As the three danced, Martin Priest sat down on a tool box and covered his face with his long hands.

They stopped, staring. Priest seemed to be in absolute despair. "What's the matter, General?" shouted the irrepressible Poodle.

The inventor raised his head and looked as though he had gone blind. "I've—I supposed—I've been hoping—but I must."

"Yes?" said Lieutenant Adeler, gently.

"I must tell you who and what I am." The inventor was grim as an officer directing a siege. Even Poodle grew quiet. Martin Priest spoke quickly, trying to get it over:

"As far as the aeroplanes go, I'm all right—I'm square. I think I am about other things, too—now, anyway. But there was a time—"

Hike walked over, as Priest stopped, and put his arm about the inventor's shoulder, for a second. The inventor smiled a three-cornered funny little smile, then looked grim again, and went on, swiftly:

"When I was a young chap—twenty-six—I married—I can't tell you what I thought of my wife, but she was perfect, to me anyway. I'd graduated from Massachusetts Tech., and was with a marine engine company. I was interested in aviation, too—long before the Wrights had flown, or the Bell people, when Lilienthal was just trying his gliders. Well, this engine company was small, and I had a lot to do with the business end of it, as well as the mechanical part. My wife got mighty sick—needed a lot of things, and my salary was small. And I got in debt for a lot of aeroplane material.

"Well, I just borrowed some money from the firm's safe—really borrowed, or that's what I thought. I was so crazy over my wife's sickness that I didn't think much about it, I guess, to tell the truth.

"They found out about it, and I was arrested, and sentenced for embezzlement.... My wife died while I was in prison—back East that was.... Convict, that's what I was. I don't know's you'll want to associate—

"Well, the warden was a fine old boy. He made me head of the machine shop. I got him interested in aviation—he was a handy man with the tools himself; and we used to do a lot of work on the side—him in Christian clothes, and me in stripes.

"When I got out I'd inherited several thousand dollars from my wife's uncle, funny old chap that had just been sitting back and watching my capers without letting me know anything about it. I wandered around the world, saw what the Wrights and Alexander Graham Bell and Curtiss were doing with aviation, and what Santos Dumont was doing in France. Saw one of J. A. D. McCurdy's first flights. Then I came out here, and built this shack, and hoped to have a machine that I could surprise the world with, just the young ranchero helping me. But now my money's practically all gone.

"Thought I'd better tell you just how things really stand with me.... I don't want any false impression—"

Hike started forward and wrung Martin Priest's hand, silently. The Lieutenant did the same. They were his friends.

As for Poodle, he did the most brilliant thing of his life—nothing at all but smile his pleasantest!

Then they began to plan the trip up to Monterey.

CHAPTER IV

THE AEROPLANE'S FIRST FLIGHT

WITH the patched Gnome engine, with Hike and Lieutenant Adeler and Martin Priest and nearly two thousand pounds of Priest's baggage, the tetrahedral *Hustle I* stood ready to start.

There is no use denying it—Hike felt a little nervous. He had flown with the Lieutenant several times, in well-tested Jolls 'planes, but with this new machine, that looked like a castle made of playing cards by some child, he was waiting to find out whether or not he was going to be scared! He didn't think he would be, but Poodle was grinning at him and declaring that he sure would be.

Martin Priest, the driver, snapped on the control. The tetrahedral's engine began racing. Down the slope in front of the aerodrome she ran, bumping and hopping, then plunged out into the air, easily as a bird. Suddenly they were two hundred feet up, crossing a foothill, rising up—up—with the elevating planes sharply tilted upward. Hike yelled with joy, for never had he felt more comfortable, more like some big eagle, than then.

The earth sank below them, and left them free of it. There was none of the jar of the smaller ordinary Jolls 'planes. The tetrahedral, though it was gaining in speed, rode as smoothly and easily as a huge steamer.

They curved over the Big Peak, and a gust of wind—a real flaw—swooped up at them from the cold valley beyond. Then they struck a "hole in the air," and the *Hustle* dropped two hundred feet. But she did not go down like a shot—she took the drop easily.

Again Hike shouted, and settled back in his seat, looking out to the blue sunny stretch of the Pacific Ocean, longing to soar over it in the *Hustle*. He laughed down at the arroyos and hills beneath them, over which they were passing so easily. They looked like small folds in a heap of green velvet.

In twenty minutes, they were in sight of Monterey. As they passed the Carmel valley, there was a crackling from the engine; it missed a stroke, and then suddenly stopped.

Hike was much interested to find that he wasn't scared, after all. Here they were, two thousand feet up, balanced on nothing but air, with the ground *very* far below, and with the engine stopped.

But Martin Priest merely turned back to him, with a grin that made his prophet face look very good-natured. Then—Martin Priest took his hands entirely off the levers, stood up, and began to sing a hymn!

Gone crazy, Hike first thought—just now, when all his skill was needed, to keep them safe on the long glide to earth! Hike's backbone seemed frozen. Then he looked at Martin Priest's face again, and down to earth. The *Hustle* was sinking as easily as a feather, with a little creaking of her many planes. Only a tetrahedral could flutter down like that.

Lieutenant Adeler stood up, made ready to grapple with Martin Priest. "Let 'im alone," shrieked Hike. "We're going all right. Part of the test."

"Good boy," Martin Priest stopped singing to say. "It is. The tetrahedral can't be wrecked." Then he stepped back to the engine, and tried her spark.

When they had softly, easily, settled down to about a hundred feet from the earth, so that the branches of trees below seemed rushing up at them, Priest yelled to the Lieutenant, "Push that right lever forward."

As the lever slid forward, Martin Priest started the engine. After the silence, it was deafening; like the crackling of a hundred machine-guns at once. Hike could scarcely hear himself, but he shouted again and again, while they darted up, then soared aloft to five thousand feet.

As they flew over Monterey, the people rushed from the streets and gardens up to the tops of their Spanish adobe houses. They were used to ordinary Jolls biplanes, but this great bird was different. On the fashionable drives and tennis-courts of the Del Monte hotel, rich Eastern tourists gazed up till their necks ached.

Hike yelled in Martin Priest's ear, "Let me try her!"

"Sure," roared back Priest, though Lieutenant Adeler, guessing what was up, shook his head. "See this lever. It raises and deflects elevating planes, for'ard there. Makes her go up and down. This one, on the left, controls her rudder—back there, like a ship's rudder. Say, I can't yell against this. Even fifty horse-power's too much."

Calmly, Priest stopped the engine. The silence sounded louder than the motor had, for a minute, and Hike yelled "Ouch!" clapping his hands to his ears.

Laughing at him, Martin Priest went on, "This bar at my feet controls the engine-feed—if you take your feet off, the feed's shut off. There aren't any ailerons, and there aren't any wings to warp, for lateral stability. (Aren't we sinking down pretty though?) Don't need them to keep from tipping, with all these little planes. The rest of the engine-control—spark and so on—is like the engine you learned on a Jolls biplane. That's enough for a first lesson. Now try her."

He started the engine, stepped back to a passenger-seat, and apparently went to sleep. Hike pushed the right lever cautiously forward, and up shot the machine—up, up, easily, swiftly, the trees and houses, spread out beneath him, fading into a mist. Then he turned in a long awkward circle, and planed easily down. He quivered as he felt the aeroplane obey him. He wanted to go on forever. He wanted to try to make a landing. But he wouldn't take any chances on wrecking the tetrahedral on her first trial trip.

So he motioned to Martin Priest to take control again, and settled back into a passenger-seat, whistling his happiness.

They landed in a field outside of Monterey. The ranchero who owned it came rushing up—and in less than ten minutes Lieutenant Adeler had bought that field from him, for an aviation-course.

Before nightfall, the Lieutenant had telegraphed to San Diego for the two hundred and thirty horse-power Kulnoch engine which, he told Martin Priest, a crank aviator down there had for sale. The lieutenant sent Hike to buy the lumber for an aerodrome, and led Martin Priest to a barber, to get his hair cut. (But Priest refused to get any better clothes. "Let all the rest of the money you want to spare go in on the tetrahedral," he said.)

Within a week, the new engine had arrived and been put into the aeroplane, while a rough shed had been built.

Then Hike heard that Captain Willoughby Welch was going to leave in a couple of days, though it was nearly a month before he was due to report to the Army Board of Aviation—which would spend a million on purchasing some sort of aeroplane. Hike and Jack Adeler had told the Captain nothing about the arrival of the Priest tetrahedral yet, wishing to surprise him after the new engine was installed.

But now Hike rushed over to the Captain's quarters, and begged him to take a look at the *Hustle*. The Captain refused, laughing in his face. The most that he would promise was to come back and take a look at her before going on to Washington. He would have to be back for a day or so, anyway, he said.

Hike was much discouraged. But he went on working with Priest and the Lieutenant. It was Hike who suggested a spring for the throttle-foot-bar, so that the aviator could take his feet off the bar, if he wished.

The Lieutenant had to go up to Benicia Arsenal, to inspect some wireless material for Army transports. This, decided Martin Priest, would be a good time for him to drive down to his valley in the San Francisquito mountains, and get some belongings. So Hike and Poodle were left alone. They slept at the aerodrome, to protect the tetrahedral from sight-seers. All the while, Hike was looking for a good excuse to fly her.

CHAPTER V

THE WRECK OF THE YACHT

HIKE was seated by the *Hustle* one windy afternoon, finishing rewinding the fastening of a small interior strut, or prop, when Poodle came rushing up, returning from town.

"Hike," he cried, "there's a yacht going to pieces down the coast. Belongs to a rich guy that lives at Pacific Grove. She's sending out an S.O.S. by wireless. The Presidio wireless caught it. Her operator says she ran onto a ledge down near Sur—how far is that? About twenty miles down the coast? There's big swells after that storm yesterday, and they can't launch a boat. Besides, the yacht's stuck on a long slippery ledge that's hard to land on."

"Where's the revenue cutter?" asked Hike.

"Gone north."

"Well," said Hike, very calmly, "well, looks to me as if we'd have to save 'em—folks on yacht."

"*Us?* How?" Poodle looked disturbed.

"Haven't we got the best aeroplane in the world right here? I guess swells won't bother the *Hustle* much."

"Us—alone in an aeroplane?" wailed Poodle. "And me never been up in one any time? Jiminy, you ain't serious, are you, Hike?"

Hike looked so quiet that Poodle, much confused at the prospect, knew he *was* serious. Hike had already started filling the *Hustle's* fuel tank with gasoline, after finishing the strut-fastening while he was talking.

"Get that long rope that came on the engine," Hike ordered.

"All *right*, Geerawld," sighed Poodle. "'F I'm going to get killed, I might's well insult you while I have the chance." He trotted out and found the rope, singing "Geerawld, brave HEro, brave HEro," in a most cheerful manner. He was frightened at the prospect of his first aeroplaning, with so young an aviator as Hike, but once he admitted that, he stopped worrying about it, and wanted to get the first part of the ride over.

"Coil the rope there—uh—well—amidships," said Hike. "Come on, now —shove!"

Perspiring and grunting, with their feet slipping on the turf floor of the aerodrome, they pushed out the big machine, then stood resting.

"Scared?" quizzed Hike.

"Uh huh."

"Well, I'll tell you now—you'd better know it if you're going up with me. I've been running this tetrahedral for a week. Priest and I kept it quiet because the Lieutenant thinks I'm too young to run one, and Father'd be scared blue if he knew I was doing it. I don't want to frighten him, and so I want to be a good, safe, crackerjack aviator before he knows. So keep still about this flight. But don't worry. Why, one night—dark night, too—I flew this thing clear up to San Francisco—about a hundred and fifty miles the course we took—and circled over the city. And Priest never touched the levers except for a couple of minutes, while we were landing. All aboard."

"Right!" said Poodle. Very gingerly, as though he were afraid of breaking something, Poodle crawled into the passenger-seat beside the aviator's and stammered, "Gee, I don't like the promenade deck on this liner. Too narrow for playing tag."

Hike swung easily into his seat, snapped on the self-starter, and grasped the levers, shouting, "We'll be down there by one o'clock."

The machine bobbed roughly over the start, like a frightened hen with wings outspread, and launched beautifully. Hike, happy at being up in the brisk breeze and bright sunshine, hummed a little song to himself, and swung the *Hustle* southward.

Poodle held his breath and waited.

For five minutes, they followed the coast-line, at sixty miles an hour—an easy speed for the *Hustle*, with her powerful engine; then Hike struck the clutch in the second notch.

At the second speed, they whirled at a hundred miles an hour. They rocked and bumped on the air-currents coming up between cliffs. Poodle held his cap before his face, trying to catch his breath, and clung to a strut with his other hand. He was too frightened to look down at the cliffs, that rushed like a black streak beneath them, but he kept arguing with himself, "Now, Poodle, me boy, now Poodle, cheer up. You're a nice kid, Poodle, and you'll sure get a golden harp, even if you *do* get killt!"

In fifteen minutes, they were over the barren coast near Sur, and Hike made out the wrecked yacht—a long, low line of white-painted hull, with masts and stack tilting far over on the ledge where she stuck, smashed by heavy surf that was breaking over her. A man was tied to the mast-head, waving a signal flag wildly at the *Hustle*. A little group of people clung to the upper rail of the yacht, watching, waiting, chilled and wet.

Hike slowed down and let the *Hustle* hover over the wreck, looking curiously down at the white faces that peered up at him, from amid spray. A huge comber swept over them—and one man was carried away. Shrieks and wails came up to him through the thunder of the surf, as he shut off the motor for a second.

27

With a quick glance, he studied out the landing places nearby. Between the wreck and the shore there was only a wave-swept ledge of rock. The shore itself was mostly composed of sheer black cliffs that ran straight down into the water. Up these terrible walls the waves ran; up ten—fifteen —twenty feet, and crashed down again, leaving the rocks shining with water. But at one spot, the shore ran in, leaving a triangle of nearly dry beach, from which a man could climb up the cliffs to safety.

That was enough for Hike. "Let that rope hang in big loop—so—" he yelled to Poodle. "Fasten two ends to strut. Tight. Reg'lar anchor-knot. Let loop hang below machine."

As Poodle obeyed, Hike hovered directly over the wreck, in the smallest circles he could manage, and at the slowest rate he could make the *Hustle* go.

The faster an aeroplane skates over her thin crust of air—like a boy on thin ice—the safer she is. But with the *Hustle's* many planes, she could hover, like a gull over a crumb in the water.

Yelling down to the people twenty feet below, waving, he made them understand that they were to wrap themselves, one by one, in the loop of the dangling rope. Finally, as the rope swept over the deck, a tall man in a reefer caught it, sat in the loop as if it were a trapeze, and was carried out over the waves, his dangling feet kicking violently.

Keeping her speed down, Hike slowly swung across to the triangle of beach and dipped. The man slipped down his trapeze—safe! on dry land!

He yelled twice, for joy, then staggered toward the cliff and began to climb. Already Hike was circling back to the wreck. As he passed the cliff, the left end of the machine missed it by only three feet. Even Hike shuddered at the thought of what would have happened if he had run full tilt into the cliff, and crumpled up the *Hustle*.

But he drove back to the wreck, and again some one—a woman, this time, terrified, and twice missing the rope before she climbed into the trapeze—was taken ashore.

The wreck was fast breaking up, and Hike hurried as much as he could. While carrying some one, he had to take it slow, but on his return trips he hurled the *Hustle* out into the gale as though he were racing.

There were thirty persons on the wreck. As he landed the seventeenth (who was the yacht-owner) on the safe beach, he was thinking hard. Two things he had noticed; that the tide was filling up the triangle of beach, so that his passengers had to climb up out of dangerous undertow that now surged over what had been safe land; and that he had to hurry, because the fragile yacht was fast breaking up.

Yes, he had to hurry—but he didn't want to run into the cliffs he had barely missed. He thrust the elevating plane sharply up, and shot toward the top of the rock-wall so straight that the tetrahedral seemed to stand on her tail.

Poodle clutched the sides of his seat. He saw his feet up as high as his head, and felt as though he were falling backwards. He gasped, and before he had finished gasping, his heart missed a beat.

For—still standing on her tail—the *Hustle* was caught in a terrible flaw of wind, and hurled a hundred feet up into the air. A breaker had brought in a draft that, shooting up through a treacherous gap in the cliffs, became a treacherous whirlwind.

Hike's heart thumped, too. He wished that Martin Priest were at the levers. But he kept hold of himself. He turned down the elevating planes; then raised them slightly, then shot them down again; and rode over the column of lifting air into a calm space.

He swung back to the wreck, determined to make quicker work of the rest of the rescue. The waves were increasing and the yacht could not stand much more.

He beckoned Poodle, and shouted to him "Going to land on yacht. You drop off first time I circle. Here, take revolver—my back pocket. If people scared, threaten 'em. Make 'em pile planks so I can land. Make 'em get in —all of 'em—when I land. Make 'em stay quiet when I start."

"All r-r-r-right."

They circled over the yacht. Poodle, the revolver in his teeth, slid down the dangling rope and fell on the slippery sloping deck of the yacht. Along her terribly listed hull, water was running free. Poodle clung to the lower rail, pulled off his socks and his trim fashionable tan shoes, and staggered up the deck. The group of thirteen men (all the women were off) watched him curiously.

Not one, except a cabin-boy, of these people, but what was many years older than plump Poodle. Any one of the sturdy Norwegian sailors could have broken him in two. But when he yelled "Pile up these boats—tear up that wrecked wheelhouse—make landing stage for aeroplane," they jumped to obey.

With Poodle tugging at planks beside the gold-braided sailing-master and a ragged fireman in overalls, with even the cabin-boy climbing along the wet deck in his drenched white jacket, they hastily piled a rude platform, with a capstan for support.

Hike was hovering in long easy circles, overhead. When Poodle waved and shouted, Hike swung astern, and came down, with the motor stopped. Slipping and skidding on the wet planking, the *Hustle* went clean off the platform, and plunged toward the sea, while the sailors shrieked in horror. A great wave broke on the wreck, and covered the aeroplane with a cloud of spray, but through it Hike glided, started his motor, circled about, constantly rising, then again stopped his motor and planed down, easily, landing on the farther edge of the rough platform.

He was hoarse from shouting through the roar of motor and waves, but as Poodle rushed up to him, with his round face shining with gladness—and spray!—Hike croaked, "Run out planks—runway."

On blocks and boxes, the crew propped up planks along which the wheels of the *Hustle's* chassis could run in starting.

"Get 'em in—*all!*" shouted Hike.

"Get in—all of you. Fill up those three seats, and crowd on that freight-platform," bellowed Poodle.

The sailing-master was a commanding figure, even in his drenched uniform. He was large and dignified and used to ordering people about. But he came up to Poodle as though that youth owned the yacht and the sea.

"Isn't the space too small for all—?" he began respectfully.

"No! Get in. Quick All'v you!" roared Poodle, leaning back sturdily on his short plump legs. Lean, sinewy Hike grinned—tired though he was from the struggle with the winds—to see his chum taking command. The sailing-master hesitated. He looked from Poodle's chubby young face to the great flying-machine, then back, then suddenly shrugged his shoulders and roared to his crew:

"Get in there. All of you.... I'll follow them," he finished, turning back to Poodle.

Packed like herrings in a barrel, the crew clung together on the platform aft of the aviator's seat, where once two thousand pounds of Martin Priest's baggage had ridden. The sailing-master slipped into one seat, Poodle into another, and they were ready.

Hike started the engine, and the tetrahedral ran along the flimsy planks which had been laid for a runway. She bounced off them, raised, whirled out, kicked up spray, and then shot up, wavering.

Hike had never been so much on the job before in all his life. He was frightened, for fourteen lives besides his depended on him. He almost deflected the elevator, which would have sent them down into the sea. But he kicked himself into courage, and studied the air-currents made by sea and cliffs.

With all this load, and their bad start from slippery planks, the *Hustle* was wobbly and sulky. But he worked her up, up, toward the top of the cliffs, when he wanted—oh! so awfully! to let her run low. He cleared the top of the cliffs, ran down the wind, and, shutting off the motor, made a safe landing in a stretch of chaparral.

The sailing-master crawled out and silently held out his hand to Hike, then to Poodle. As he did so, the owner of the yacht rushed up, and held out his hand, too. Then there was a rush of people, while the owner's wife began to cry with relief.

"Please tell me—now—what I can do in return," began the owner. "I'm pretty well off—"

"Just two things," croaked Hike, huskily. "Keep this out of the papers—don't say how you got rescued. And then maybe some day I may come buttin' in asking you if you won't put some capital behind the inventor of this aeroplane. As a business proposition. Gee, I'm tired. I'm going to beat it back home. Come on, Poodle. Crawl in. Say, you people, I guess from the way it looks when you're way up in the aeroplane, you'll find a road about a mile east of here. I'll tell your people you're on it—have 'em send teams. So long."

Blushing at making so long a speech before so many people, Hike again started his motor, and was off for home.

CHAPTER VI

GO!

IT was the day before the date on which the Army Board of Aviation would meet at Washington—a Monday in August. Hike Griffin sat with Poodle and Martin Priest at the *Hustle's* shed. Lieutenant Adeler was still up at Benicia Arsenal.

Captain Willoughby Welch had not come back to Monterey, before starting for Washington to report on the best model of aeroplane for the Army to purchase. He had never even looked at the tetrahedral, and it was certain that he would declare to the Army Board that the Jolls—the P. J. Jolls Company's—biplanes and monoplanes were the only possible sort for the Army to purchase. The Army Board would not hear a word about the tetrahedral.

Lieutenant Adeler and Hike had both written to Welch, but he had answered merely that he would try to get back to Monterey.

Hike was talking, and Martin Priest was listening with great respect, for he had heard of Hike's rescue of the shipwrecked yacht crew. Poodle had thus described what happened after the affair:

"Well, as soon as he gets back to Pacific Grove, Mr. Man puts on a clean pair of pants and, says he, 'I will now beat it over to Monterey and call on the angel wot saved me—that angel named Geerawld, and ask him will he let me give him a toy cart to play with.' He finds Priesty here, and, says he, 'Priest,' says he, 'young Hike is a' angel.' Priesty, knowing him better, 'lows that Hike ain't a angel, but a chimpanze-faced spoon-cat, as orders his pleasant young friend Torrington Darby around something scandalous. Also he 'lows that it was li'l Torry that really saved the wrecked crew, like he was in a moving picture show.

"But Mr. Man tells Priesty that Hike done it all, and now that horrid Hike had cer-tain-ly got Priesty going.

"'Stick your engine out on the end of your um-dee-diddle,' says Hike, 'so's it'll get more purchase on the bizangus.' 'Yessir, right away, sir,' says Priesty and—"

That was as far as Poodle ever got with his description of the meeting between the yacht-owner and Martin Priest, for one Hike Griffin rose, just then, with a strut in his hand, and Poodle found pressing business elsewhere. No doubt Poodle's description didn't follow the facts exactly, but it is certain that after that meeting with the yacht-owner, Martin Priest declared Hike could handle the tetrahedral as well as he—Priest—could ever hope to.

Now Priest was listening eagerly, while Hike said:

"Well, if Wibbelty-Wobbelty has gone to Washington, the only way we can get a hearing before the Army Board is to take the tetrahedral there. Even then Wibbelty will try to spoil the game, but we can show the goods."

"Gee, you talk awful ungrammatical-like," yawned Poodle, from a comfortable position on the grass.

"The Lieutenant's tried his best to get an opening to report before the Board," Hike went on, "but Dad's still got the idea the tetrahedral won't work, and he won't recommend the Lieutenant's application for a chance to talk and so I guess the Loot's got pretty sore, and is just planning to put all his own money behind our—your, I mean—tetrahedral, and let the government's money go hang. I don't think we ought to let him do that, do you, Mr. Priest?"

"No, I don't," said Martin Priest, sadly, shaking his head.

"Well, then," said Poodle, "why don't you take the *Hustle* to Washington, Mr. Priest, and show her to the Board?"

"No, no. I couldn't do that," Martin Priest exclaimed. "I'd be—oh, I don't know. I suppose it was my experience in prison, but I'd be afraid of all those gold-laced kings. I feel that if they want my machine—it's a good machine, I've done my work on it—it's up to them to come and inspect it. If your Captain Welch wouldn't even look at it—why, what chance would I have with a general?"

"Rats!" sniffed Poodle. "I'll bet the General's twice as easy a man to talk to as that snortling Willoughby-Walloughby."

"He sure is," said Hike. "He stayed with Dad for two days once, at Rock Island Arsenal. Old friend of Dad's. He's awf'ly nice, General Thorne is."

"No, no, no!" insisted Martin Priest. "I couldn't face that Board. They'd get me angry, and I'd spoil all my chances for—"

He ceased. All three kept silent. Outside the aerodrome, the sunset glowed. Hike was tramping about uneasily, looking at the reflection of the gold and crimson, in the east. Suddenly he said to Poodle:

"See that light. Pretty, ain't it?"

"Classy sunset," declared Poodle, dreamily. Hike suspected that, in spite of Poodle's slang, he was planning a poem. Poodle had once had a poem in the Santa Benicia school paper, and no one knew but that he might break out that way again.

Suddenly Hike said, "Sure is great. And we'll see it nearer. Pood', we're going to sail right into that light there in the east. *We're going to take the* Hustle *to Washington!* Do you hear, Mr. Priest? Poodle and I are going to go and interview that Army Board. Thirty hours from now we'll be there. Got enough gasoline and oil for three thousand miles?"

"Yes!" Priest was shouting with excitement.

"Fill her tanks. Poodle, I'll write a note to Father saying where we're gone—you take it up to the house. I'll get the grub for the trip and pack her aboard."

Hike was the only calm one of the three.

"All right. Great!" Poodle yelled, while Martin Priest hurried to fill the *Hustle's* fuel-tank.

In half an hour, Martin Priest stood at the door of the aerodrome, looking to the east at a moving black spot. The tetrahedral was disappearing into the gray sky, with Hike at the levers.

Poodle was used to aviating, now. He was whistling quite carelessly and busily packing the food snugly away, and lighting the tetrahedral's search-light, like a sailor coiling ropes as a schooner pulls out from her moorings, as the *Hustle* soared up to pass over the Coast Range.

CHAPTER VII

A GLIDE TO SAFETY

THE *Hustle* was hurling herself through the night at a hundred miles an hour. The roar of the great Kulnoch motor filled the air; and through it sounded a sharp whine as the wind struck the planes. The powerful searchlight bored a hole through intense darkness ahead, now and then showing a mountain peak; at sight of which Hike shot the machine up so fast that she seemed about to turn turtle. Sometimes the light, turned down on earth, picked out a mining town, with everyone asleep; sometimes, a broad river, shining in the light, between threatening rock walls.

On the *Hustle* dashed, never hesitating, over valleys and patches of yellow desert, from which a warm wind rose to flutter the planes; over hills and forests and long railroad-trestles where rails flashed in the light.

Hike had to think about a hundred things, but most of all he thought about keeping the *Hustle* going *on*—on to Washington—on to save Martin Priest! This was no time to lose his nerve or his wits. On; no matter how much his eyes smarted and watered in the wind. On; though his hands got cold and cramped, as they clutched the levers; and he seemed deaf for life, in the ceaseless smashing sound of the motor. He had to make the *Hustle* hustle!

He remembered a hundred parts of the machine all at once. He studied out where he was, on a map that unrolled from one rod upon another, and avoided bad hill-passes. He kept an eye on the dial of his aneroid barometer, strapped to his wrist like a watch. The barometer showed how high they were, and he never let the machine drop below two thousand feet, if he could help it; and so avoided the bad air-currents near earth. He watched the engine feed, tried the carbureter, saw that the fuel-mixture was right. He looked back at the rudder, and saw that it answered his lever. Most of all, he studied his roadway—the air.

Though he was heading as due east as possible, a powerful north wind was driving him southward before it. Sometimes the wind, suddenly charging from a great gap between two mountain peaks, tossed the *Hustle* like a leaf; picked it up and threw it almost against a hill; then let it drop two hundred feet.

The sailor of small boats is rather busy, among heavy seas, when a sudden flaw of wind strikes his sail. He has to keep the tiller on the jiggle, watch the mainsail, and be ready to let go the mainsheet almost before he can think. But sailing a small boat is as much easier than driving an aeroplane through uneven air-currents as sliding down hill is easier than sailing.

Hike had always to be ready to coax the *Hustle* up again, when she struck an air-pocket and fell like an elevator with a broken cable. He had to guess at what sort of currents were ahead of him, and be ready to round each tiny whirlwind as soon as he felt it slap at the planes.

He was too busy to be frightened, ever. Poodle had more time for that. Poodle kept the aeronautical map moving from one roller to another; he swung the search-light's glare from hill to valley, and looked after the flow of oil from its tank to the distributing pipes, but mostly he sat there and watched the world jump up at them from below. Half a dozen times, when they seemed to be dashing down to the rocky ground, he felt quite certain they were killed, and wondered how he could jump and save himself. Just the same, he kept up a grin, for Hike to see when he glanced back, and, whenever Poodle slapped his arms to keep warm, he tried to be as cheery a clown as possible, so that "good ole Hike'll have somethin' 'appy to look at." He busied himself with heating some coffee and broth, on the electric stove at the side of the platform, and made Hike gulp down a little of it. It was a bit curious to look down from the bubbling aluminum coffee-pot to a valley a thousand feet below, glaring in the search-light.

When the sky grew light with dawn, in front of them, and the hills looked cheerless in the early gray, Hike called Poodle to the seat beside him, and gave him the last of several lessons in aviation. Finally, he let Poodle drive her, for a while. Leaning against a pile of blankets and food on the platform, he stretched out his cramped legs, for a short rest.

The clouds promised rain and a bad wind, so Hike soon took the levers again. He made out by his map, soon after dawn, that they were over Kansas. They were coming to the end of the hilly country, into the plains; speeding over a hundred miles an hour. Hike was just planning to push her up to a hundred and fifty an hour when he made out something that caused him to swoop closer to earth, and hastily slow her down, with his foot-throttle. The shock almost threw Poodle out of his seat, and sent a can of coffee hurtling across the freight-platform.

Hike had seen a man and woman, ahead of them, riding madly across a stretch of prairie, toward a river. Pursuing them were a dozen men, also on horseback, shouting and shooting. The man and woman were not over half a mile ahead, and the pursuers were gaining.

Hike dropped, stopped his motor, landed just ahead of the fleeing couple, on a butte overlooking a deep narrow cut through which a river, swollen by recent rain, was raging. As the *Hustle* landed, the storm broke out in thunder.

The fleeing couple galloped up, shouting through the rain, "Help us!"

"What's matter?" cried Poodle. "Get aboard!"

"Horse-thieves—there—kidnapped young lady—my sweetheart—wanted make her marry man—I got her back—they want lynch me," panted the man, as he vaulted from his horse. He helped down the girl and lifted her on the freight-platform of the *Hustle*. He was a clean, decent-looking chap, Hike thought, and the story was probably true, with those wild bandits chasing the couple.

Hike switched on the spark—but the engine did not start. Through the rain the pursuers could be seen, galloping toward them. A rifle bullet sang through the *Hustle's* planes.

"What's matter?" Poodle yelled again.

Hike shouted, "Dunno—won't start. Climb out—we'll *glide* across river!"

They pushed the machine to the down slope of the butte, toward the river, and swung back into their seats. Down the slope she ran, rose a little, and glided out into the air, over the river.

But their start had been bad. The ground had been wet, their shove short. The *Hustle* was settling down, threatening to drop into the river. They had to rise, to get over the hilly bank on the other side.

Thinking it all out, in a second, while they were soaring, Hike decided to lighten their load. "Deflect elevating plane when get over!" he howled to Poodle, and then leaped from his seat, out into the air, and dropped down into the river.

He was badly shaken up, but he crawled out on the farther bank, and rushed up the hilly river-edge. He saw the *Hustle* sail across the river, just grazing the hill, and then disappear beyond the hill, safe. On the side of the river from which they had just come, the pursuing men had already ridden up to the top of the butte. Hike hastened to the safely stopped machine and, diving down beside her engine, tried the spark.

Poodle climbed out and stood on guard, with his revolver ready.

"Gwan up the hill. See they don't ford river," said Hike, and Poodle, his plump legs going like bicycle-wheel spokes, dashed up to the rise overlooking the water.

In the rain that pelted the river till its surface looked like little hills and valleys, and soaked him to the skin, Poodle lay on his stomach atop the hill, and watched the pursuers stop, take council, then ride down to the water and put their frightened horses at the rushing river.

He didn't want to shoot—he didn't want to take a chance of killing any one, reflected soft-hearted young Poodle. But he looked back at the frightened young man and woman who, from their seats in the *Hustle*, were watching Hike work over the engine, seeming even more frightened by the fight than interested in their first aeroplane.

Then he looked back at the pursuers, grimly; took aim at the big black-bearded man who led the bunch, and shouted down, "Halt!"

The man, urging his horse into the river, looked up, amazed, then grinned to see a boy trying to keep *him* back! He didn't know that the boy, instead of being frightened, was doing some grinning himself, thinking, "Gee—wish he didn't look so much like Martin Priest—but here goes. Going to be a surprise-party, right here." He shot at the leader's horse three times, paused, saw the animal topple over into the river, and then began firing at the horses of the others—sorry for the animals, but never stopping pumping lead into them.

But the men were like savages. While he was firing at one section, another bunch rode down a little farther along, and began to ford. Then Poodle heard a "Bang, bang, bang!" near him, and saw the young man whom they were rescuing lying on his stomach, holding a revolver.

The young man seemed happy, now that he was in action. Stopping only to yell, "The Cap'n, yonder, ordered me on the firing line," he began to shoot without stopping.

But their revolvers were not good for the long range, and it would have taken Gatling guns to stop that crowd of desperate cattle-rustlers.

The black-bearded leader had run back up the bank, across the river. He mounted the horse which the young man had abandoned when he got in the tetrahedral. Again he was fording, yelling like a wild man.

Some of the bunch were across. Poodle and the young man ran back to the *Hustle*, and continued firing from its shelter as the horse-thieves circled about, discharging their rifles. Hike kept working as calmly and swiftly over the engine as though he were in the aerodrome.

Suddenly the bandits turned and galloped away, as an infernal cracking, like a Gatling gun, came from the *Hustle*. Hike had started the engine.

"Quick, in!" shouted Hike, and the three swung into their seats. The *Hustle* ran, darted up and they soared, over the heads of the bandits, who shot at them wildly and vainly.

The machine never stopped till she had reached the young man's town, fifty miles farther on. There they descended in the town-park, the young man and his rescued lady climbed out, and started to thank Hike and Poodle.

But about the time they had got out three words, they stopped, for the *Hustle* was darting away over the town, at a hundred and fifty miles an hour, to make up time.

"Them's nice boys," said the young man.

"Lovely," said the young lady. "They must be going awful far in that contraption—maybe as far as Chicago!"

CHAPTER VIII

A FIGHT IN THE SKY

A HUNDRED and fifty miles an hour!

It takes nerve not to slow down when, for hours at a time, the earth rushes so fast and so far beneath you that hills and towns and fields all blur together in one brown smear, and you don't know where you would land if there were an accident suddenly. It takes nerve to see a city far off, then suddenly have it spread all about beneath you, with dangerous currents swirling up between its buildings, and then have it vanish behind you. But they had to make up time. They were late. Hike had to keep his grit.

He was getting nervous and tired from his long strain. Each time he swung the rudder, he jerked at his weary backbone, too. He had to keep telling himself foolish little things, to remain calm. "He mustn't let good ole Poodle get hurt" thought Hike. "This would soon be over.... Be over.... Another hour, and he'd take a rest....: Bimeby, he'd slow down to a safe easy slow hundred an hour.... Anyway, if anything happened, the *Hustle* would probably sink safely to earth.... Besides, there was the stabilisator to depend on."

The stabilisator is a mechanism which controls the rudder and elevating planes by means of sliding weights and plates of metal, and all by itself brings the machine back to an even keel if she tips too much. Hike took a lot of comfort in thinking about the stabilisator. He did not worry, but kept the *Hustle* whirling on, at a hundred and fifty an hour.

It was about noon that they were passing over the Tennessee mountains, toward which the north wind had driven them, out of their course. About twelve-thirty, perhaps a quarter of an hour later, Hike decided that the rudder was not answering the lever properly. It looked as though the fastening of the rudder-control-wire was working loose under the terrific twitches he had been giving it.

Far ahead, there was a broad hill, among the wild, wooded mountains. He slowed down, dipped toward the hill, circled it, and made out a broad bare space, on which he finally landed. Slowly, he crawled out of his seat, and reached the ground. He found himself so dizzy and stiff that he promptly sat down on the grass and stared dumbly at the tetrahedral, rubbing his tired wrists, slowly.

Poodle, waked up by the stopping of the machine, yawned till it looked as though the top of his head would come off, scratched his left ear, and grunted:

"Gee, you're lazy. Ain't I been teaching you in-dus-try and habits of work? And what d'you do? Here I get to thinking, kinda deep, about how I can improve your character, and then you go and sneak in a sleep on me. It's orful."

"Yuh," said Hike meekly. "Well, I'll try to do better."

"That's wery comfortin', Geerawld, and so I'll just go to sleep again."

"You *will* not. You'll help me fix the rudder."

"Why didn't you have the brakeman call me at our last stop, and I'd have fixed it for you. What's the trouble? Is the doodingers cross-circuited with the bezingelum? Well, just switch on the other gallywoggs, and that will make it all right."

"No, the trouble is," stated Hike, very seriously, "that the bezingelum is getting charged by contact with the ornithigulus."

"Oh, I see. Then I suppose I'll have to stop that deep *thinking* I was telling you about, and show you how to fix it."

Poodle crawled out, and sat down beside Hike. They said nothing, but stretched themselves out on the dry grass. Soon, there was a sound of deep, slow breathing. In half an hour, Hike awoke—to find that they had been asleep!

Dragging the unfortunate Poodle to the *Hustle*, he made him hold wires and pliers, while he tightened the fastening of the rudder. While he worked, he glanced at the valleys and mountains about them.

He exclaimed, "Gee! Say, Poodle, get your gun ready again. There's a guy—"

"A *what*?"

"Hush! Quick. Man's crawling up the hillside, with a long rifle that looks like business. I wonder what—"

From the nearest clump of bushes suddenly came a harsh loud voice:

"Well, you young fellers won't wonder long! You-all better come with me."

A tall man in home-spun, tall, gaunt, fierce as a wild beast, was covering them with his rifle. From the other bushes rose a dozen men, young and old, all savage as the first mountaineer.

Hike started to explain that the tetrahedral was not an anarchist machine or anything like that, but the first man bade him to "Shut up!"

The hill where the *Hustle* had landed was the center of a camp of moon-shiners, who had been driven from their stills by a big raid by revenue officers. They had fled here, with rifles, bags of corn-meal, bacon and whiskey, and were waiting for the revenue officers to try to creep in on them from the mountains about. When they had seen the tetrahedral swoop down, they had immediately thought it a new method of the "revenuers," and they believed the boys—too young to be officers—treacherous spies.

So much Hike gathered from their threats and sneers. He saw that Poodle and he must either escape or be lynched. Poodle, who was looking around in a scared way at the scowling ring of men with ready rifles, was not too scared to whisper, "We'd better beat it. We'll be late in getting to Washington you know, if we get lynched."

Hike had a plan. Addressing the leader, he explained that they had nothing to do with the revenue officers, and that he would prove it if the leader would step into the machine and examine their papers.

Very suspicious, the leader refused to do more than approach. He demanded to see the papers outside. Hike leaned over a storage battery, and suddenly the leader stood as stiff as though he had been turned to marble.

For the first time, Hike had used the Paralyzing Wave!

It was an invention of Priest's, by which a wave, thrown out from an electrical device, stiffened the victim at whom the wave was aimed, for several minutes.

The crowd stared at the leader. Hike walked up and cried, "What is the matter?" Turning to the other moonshiners, he cried, "Help me. Your leader has been overcome by bedingulus bubulus."

They looked with suspicious wonder at him. But a boy who could run a thing like this "flyin' machine," and could use such long words must know something about it; and this sudden disease was certainly mysterious.

They helped the paralyzed leader into the tetrahedral. Their rifles were laid aside, and they were much impressed at the manner in which Hike and Poodle stirred strange liquids in a cup and poured the mixture down the paralyzed leader's throat.... If they had known that the mixture was of lubricating oil and liquid wing-sheathing (for repairs), they would not have been so respectful.

While apparently working over the leader, Hike suddenly started the engine, and before the mountaineers could more than reach their rifles, the great tetrahedral had rushed down the slope, and was off, sailing through the air, carrying away the insensible leader.

The moonshiners began to fire. Bullets, shot true, pierced the planes. Hike was protected by the motor, but Poodle, behind him, suddenly squeaked, as a .44-40 bullet struck his left shoulder, tore through; and the shoulder smarted as though a terrible red-hot iron had been bored into it.

Hike had not heard him, did not know he was struck. Turning his back, Poodle pulled off his coat, and wrapped a handkerchief about the shoulder, using his teeth and right hand. The wound was not deep, though it was bleeding, and Poodle was glad that he had not been "killt entirely." He pulled on his coat again, and tried to look as though he had not been hurt at all, watching the stupefied leader, still lying motionless on the freight-platform.

Hike took the *Hustle* over the next range of mountains, turned her somewhat northward, through a broad valley where the air-currents were safe, and beckoned to Poodle. "Here—take her through this valley. About time for Mr. Man to wake up, and there'll be a fight. Be ready to switch the motor off when I kick you in the back. (No, I won't kick hard!) Then take her on as long a glide as you can—keep her up for quite a while."

Poodle felt the sting of his arm, and the sickening sensation of loss of blood, too much to make one of his customary answers. He took the driver's seat, keeping the injured shoulder away from Hike. Though it seemed as though he was wrenching his injured left arm out, every time he moved it, he forced himself to handle the levers and keep the *Hustle* at ninety miles an hour.

Hike climbed back to where the leader lay. The man was just stirring, opening his eyes dully. Hike covered him with the revolver of the *Hustle's* warlike crew, and peacefully waited.

The effects of the electrical current passed quickly away, and the mountaineer sat up. His grim, set face—the face of a man who had fought all his life—showed that he was not afraid even of his first ride in an aeroplane—and certainly not of a revolver in the hands of a boy.

He shouted, "Lay that gun down, or I'll throw you off this flyin'-machine. Then make that fat boy there take me down and let me off."

Hike answered, smiling, "Louder, my dear man, motor makes so much noise."

"Hear me?" cried the man. "I'll take that gun away from you. You couldn't get in more'n one shot before I grabbed you—and you couldn't get in that. I know you-all's sort. You'd try to shoot, but you ain't got the grit to shoot down a man, this near, in cold blood. If I have to take that gun away from you, I'll throw you off. Better let me down peaceful, and save your life."

Hike knew that the man was right in saying that he would not care to shoot a man two feet from him. But even so, he was not going to lay down the revolver.

It was a test of nerves. They argued back and forth, Hike merely throwing in a few words, never taking his calm cold gray eyes from the steely, snake-like eyes of the moonshiner. The latter's nerves were getting a little shaky, especially at having to yell and listen in this infernal racket made by the motor. He was used to the quiet mountains.

Hike watched him get ready to spring, then he touched Poodle's back with his toe, and a sudden great silence was about them, as the motor was shut off. At the same time, Hike touched a strut, quickly.

The mountaineer, surprised, shrank back and grabbed at the sides of the freight-platform, fearing that an accident had happened.

Hike spoke, clearly and quickly:

"My dear sir, you're perfectly correct in thinking I am bluffing, with this revolver. Don't care to shoot you. But also, you're bluffing. You know if you threw me overboard you'd never get to earth alive. Look down there. If you make one single move, I'll kick this dynamite-exploder, and the whole machine will go to pot. You noticed that when I touched this wooden rod, here, I stopped the engine. You notice we're falling through the air, now. We'll all be killed unless I turn on the power—and I'm the only one that knows how."

With all this confusion of "dynamite-exploder" (which was really only a harmless timer) and "stopping engines" and "falling through the air," the mountaineer, seeing the earth rapidly swooping up at them, as Poodle made her glide over a hill, lost his steely nerve, and begged for mercy. Never had he met a boy of sixteen who played thus with life and death.

Smiling quietly, Hike slouched to the engine and switched her on, from the auxiliary connection.

As the machine resumed her regular course again, the man made several attempts to regain his nerve, but each time he moved Hike made as though to kick the timer, and the frightened leader subsided.

They had been sailing for half an hour, when Hike yelled forward to Poodle, "Take her down."

The *Hustle* landed in a hill-pasture, and, with a very courtly gesture, Hike motioned the mountaineer to step out. With his revolver covering him all the time, Hike bade him good-by.

The man crawled out and ran, never looking back.

Watching him, Hike said, "Well, I'm ashamed of myself, now it's over—taking that poor duffer fifty miles away from home just to get even. And making you take the levers, Poodle. Regular kid way, ain't it—"

He turned toward the machine, and then cried out with sorrow and amazement. For Poodle did not hear him. As soon as they had landed, Poodle had fainted, and the blood from his wound was turning all his left shoulder red.

CHAPTER IX

TWO BOYS AND A GENERAL

TEARING off Poodle's coat, ripping up his shirt sleeve. Hike found that the wound was not very deep, but that some blood had been lost. With quick, careful fingers, he bathed the wound with water from a spring, never ceasing to keep an eye on the mountaineer—who was not stopping, however, but still on the run.

Poodle opened his eyes, and, as Hike started to heap all sorts of blame on himself, grinned:

"That's the time I fooled you, all right, heh?"

"Gee, Poodle—I want to kill myself. I didn't know you were hurt. It was a crime, my keeping the game up. I wanted to get our warlike friend good and frightened before we dropped him, so he wouldn't fight afterwards. But lots of it was just fool fun—I could have used the Paralyzing Wave again. But I thought it would do him good to learn a lesson about butting in on aeroplanes. Gee, I'm awf'ly sorry, Poodski, I'd—"

"I got you going now, all right!" chuckled Poodle. "I'll keep you nice— and—humble, now, Cap'n.... Cut it out, Hike, I know you didn't know I was shot. And I wasn't—much. I'll be all right, now you got the thing tied up. Beat it for Washington."

"Think you can stand—"

"Say, you going to treat me like a little kid?" shrieked Poodle, pretending to be much hurt and insulted. "Think I can't stand a little scratch?"

Hike apologized, helped Poodle in, and started the *Hustle*, while Poodle, in his seat, grinned all over at thinking of how easily he had made Hike "cut out the weeps and lemme 'lone and tend to flyin'-machining."

Though they passed over some thousands of people, who stared up at their strange machine, the boys had no more unfortunate accidents. Just before dawn, that night, they stopped, in a field just outside of Washington, D. C., their journey practically over—and their fuel mostly gone.

Once the *Hustle* had landed, two hustlers changed into very tired and somewhat cross boys. There was a slight drizzle. They were too tired to light the alcohol-stove and cook anything, though they were hungry enough, to quote Poodle, "to eat the wheels off'n the chassis." So they nibbled at tablets of condensed food, crawled into blankets, and disconsolately dozed, feeling as little like heroes of the air as though they had been merely sailing a boat five miles.

It was nearly dawn before they got to sleep. When Hike woke, after only five hours' rest, he still felt weary and "grouchy." He reckoned by his watch (still set for Pacific Coast time) that it must be almost nine, and rushed down to the Potomac River, near which they were landed. A crowd of farmers had gathered, staring at the boys as though they had dropped from Mars. Hike paid no attention to them, but, slipping behind a big plane tree, pulled off his clothes and dashed into the river.

There he splashed till he felt awake again; then sallied out, and persuaded the farmers to leave them in peace. He bought some gasoline at an automobile station, filled the *Hustle's* tank, made coffee on the portable stove, and awoke Poodle.

The latter sprang up, trying hard to look as though he "felt like a kink," as, he insisted, he did feel. His injured shoulder was very stiff, but promised to be well in a couple of days—well enough for Poodle to pretend that it was all right, at least! He danced about in his favorite Highland Fling, and managed to look very much unlike a wounded aviator.

Hike, though, had grown serious. He had to face the Army Board of Aviation—and that very morning. Poodle said Hike looked "as if he'd found three hairs on his chin, and wanted to be real' grown-up, to match his big beard!"

Breakfast finished, they packed, and Hike wearily took the *Hustle* up, circled over Washington, and landed in the grounds of the White House, across from the State, War, and Navy Building. From what he had heard his father tell of Washington, and from what he had seen of it as a child, on a visit, he was sure that the Army Board of Aviation would be meeting here; with Captain Willoughby Welch telling how fine the P. J. Jolls aeroplane was.

Leaving the tetrahedral, around which a crowd was already gathering, in Poodle's charge, Hike hurried across to the War Building, and found the Board's meeting room. He gave a note to the orderly at the door.

* * * *

General Thorne, commander of the Signal Corps, was hiding a yawn, as he listened to Captain Welch's long report. An orderly brought him a note from the son of his old friend Major James Griffin. The General remembered young Jerry Griffin perfectly, remembered his lean strong young body and his courteous seriousness; and when he read that Jerry was there, with "something very important that I must tell you, *right away*, about the Monterey tests of aeroplanes," he stepped out to the anteroom, and greeted Hike warmly. Hike's eyes flashed joy as he saw the kindliness on the ruddy face of the little dried-up, gray-haired, bright-eyed General.

"Glad to see you, Gerald. Your father here with you?"

"No, sir. It's like this. Captain Welch—he's been reporting on the Jolls aeroplanes? Has he mentioned Priest's tetrahedral?"

"I couldn't very well tell you the content of his report, my boy. But I can say that he hasn't said anything about *any* kind of a tetrahedral."

"He should have, sir, because Lieut ——, one of the officers at Monterey, has been making some experiments with a new tetrahedral sort of aeroplane, on the side, and he's found it a lot the best aeroplane in the world."

The General smiled. "Don't you suppose Captain Welch would mention it, if that were the case—and I know he won't because he gave an outline of what his report would be before he started making it. I think you must have been a little fooled about this wonderful new aeroplane of yours, Jerry."

"Why, General Thorne, that tetrahedral could fly from San Francisco to Washington—say three thousand miles, a little over, maybe—at a hundred and fifty to two hundred miles an hour, without a stop, carrying all its fuel, and a thousand or two thousand pounds of freight or explosives or passengers!"

"Well, well, that would be quite a feat—but I'm afraid it couldn't be done, Jerry."

"Well, it *has* made the trip in about thirty hours—regular rate of a hundred miles an hour, and going at two hundred an hour when it wanted to. Got a gear-change, you see," declared Hike.

"It has? Well, why didn't I hear about this wonderful flight, pray? When was it made, and who was the aviator?" The General evidently thought there was something the matter with the mind of "Major Griffin's boy." Also he seemed to be in a hurry to get back to the meeting of his Board. His smile was kindly but rather hurried.

"Oh, the flight was just finished. Thirty hours. Monterey to here. I was the aviator! And the tetrahedral is resting itself over in the White House grounds, now! If you'll come to a window that overlooks it, I'll show you!"

The General forgot all about the meeting of the Aviation Board, and hurried to a window, from which they could see the great tetrahedral, resting like a nesting hen, with Poodle busily refusing to answer questions put to him by a great crowd, which the police were trying to keep back.

"There she is, just here from Monterey. Arrived late last night." Hike had to grin at the bewilderment on the General's face. "If you and the Board will come up to the roof, I'll drive that tetrahedral in circles all over Washington, at two hundred miles an hour. Then we'll see if Mr. Captain Welch oughtn't to mention—"

"Respect toward him till he's proven remiss, Jerry," warned the General. "But I'm sure we'll be glad to come up and see you fly. Well, well, *well*!

Two hundred miles an hour! And a boy like you! Well, *well*! But Jerry, are you sure it's safe? I wouldn't want Jim Griffin's son to get hurt— Well, if you came clear from Monterey—"

So the General herded his Board of Aviation to the roof of the State, War, and Navy Building. Captain Willoughby Welch, his report interrupted, very indignant and amazed, followed them.

Hike had hurried down to the White House grounds. It took him ten minutes to persuade the policemen handling the crowd gathered about the *Hustle* that he had a right to get up near her; but once he had edged to her, he swung himself in and started the engine. The crowd scattered in fear.

"Going two hundred an hour. And over buildings—bum currents between buildings. You watch the engine," Hike directed Poodle, who drawled back, "Did they make you a general while you were up in the war shack, or only a colonel?"

Hike took her up easily. Even at fifty miles an hour, they seemed to be "going some," as they rushed over business blocks and church steeples. But he quickly shoved her up to a hundred—a hundred and fifty—two hundred miles an hour. They were now over the Capitol grounds, then almost instantly way out over Georgetown, whirling with breath-taking speed along the Potomac, then making a couple of huge but dismayingly quick circles over the Washington Monument. At first, in the bad air-drafts, the *Hustle* tossed like a small boat in a blow, but Hike climbed up to four thousand feet, where the *Hustle*, with her great expanse of planes, ran fairly steadily and smoothly.

Hike suddenly began making great circles about the whole city, smaller circles and higher each time, so that the *Hustle's* path was like a corkscrew. Up and up he dashed, to twelve thousand feet; climbing much quicker than one could in the unsteady ordinary biplanes. Once up at that magnificent height, from which he could see, through a slight mist, the capital city spread out like a dim map, he stopped the motor, and came volplaning down like a lazy butterfly, till he was within five hundred feet of the crowd atop the State, War, and Navy Building.

Then came the really great test. Starting her engine, he floated over the central part of the city at about the slowest rate ever made by an aeroplane —keeping her down, for a time, to fifteen miles an hour. No aeroplane except a tetrahedral can go really slow without falling; and this easy pace was the thing which made General Thorne, watching through a field-glass up there on the War Building, squeal with delight, like a nice gray old mouse. Forgetting his rank, he clapped Captain Willoughby Welch joyously on the shoulder.

Captain Wibbelty-Wobbelty wasn't so glad, somehow, as the General.

Suddenly Hike shot her up again, shut off the motor, and *took his hands off the levers*. The tetrahedral began falling, slowly, easily.

Never in his life had Hike wanted to do anything so much as to seize those levers, and guide her safely down, but he made himself keep his hands off, though Poodle was shrieking, "What's matter?" This was the last great test. The tetrahedral was the only model that could safely flutter down by herself—like a great box-kite.

He touched the levers only once, to guide the aeroplane into an open spot in the White House grounds. It was the *Hustle* herself that finally settled down, with a jar which shook up the young aviators, but did no harm. As they crawled out, General Thorne was already rushing up, in a government automobile, and fairly spluttering his admiration as he grabbed for Hike's hand.

"My boy, my *boy*! Well, *well*, WELL, WELL! Greatest flight in the world. The Army's got to have your tetrahedral! Want you to come right up to the Board room. Just a minute and soldiers will be here to guard your machine. Let me look her over, meanwhile. And this is—? Mr. Torrington Darby? Glad to meet— Oh, better known as Poodle, eh! Well, God bless you, my boy, whatever your name is. You two boys will go down in history."

"Gee, I hope not," breathed Poodle. "It's bad enough to have to study history now, without having to study about *us*. Gee—think of the history master saying to me, 'Darby, recite on how the great Darby first got famous.' Be awful, General—don't you see, I'd have to say, 'By hanging onto Geerawld Griffin's coat tails.' Ouch!"

As they talked, a file of soldiers bored through the newly gathered crowd and formed about the *Hustle*. Returning the corporal's salute, General Thorne led the boys to the automobile, and they were whirled off to the State, War, and Navy Building.

The whole Board wanted to hear a full report on the tetrahedral, and they wanted to hear it immediately. But who was to make it? Even the captured General Thorne admitted that Hike seemed too young a person for that.

"Lieutenant Adeler, stationed at Monterey, knows all about the tetrahedral," suggested Poodle modestly, while Hike echoed, "Yes—he's just the person."

"Very well—but this Board can't very well wait a week or ten days for him to get here," said General Thorne.

"I'll bring him here in thirty to forty hours from now, if you'll telegraph him his orders to report here, and be waiting for me at Benicia Arsenal (he's there, just now) when I get there, so I won't miss him," shouted Hike, excitedly, seeing success for the *Hustle* and Martin Priest.

"How bring him? By the tetrahedral? Great—that will be the final test! And I'll ask Captain Welch to go with—" began the General.

Then he turned to Captain Welch who, in the farthest corner of the room, was scowling and glowering, as though he had just lost a battle. As he looked at the Captain, General Thorne's nice eyes suddenly grew cold, and he went on, sarcastically:

"Or no. I remember that Captain Welch was so busy investigating Jolls aeroplanes that he couldn't take time to look into this tetrahedral, even though it was right there at Monterey. I think we'll have Captain Welch relieved from further duty in this matter. I'll ask you, Major Tomkins, to go with this young man—Major Tomkins, Mr. Gerald Griffin—in the tetrahedral, and make a careful study of its working during its trip to California and back. Please regard him as completely in charge of it, however. And Mr. Jerry—did you tell me that Mr.—Mr. Priest, is it?—the inventor—is at Monterey? Bring him here, too, if he'll come. Good-by, and God bless you, my boy!"

While Signal Corps mechanics were looking over the *Hustle* to make sure that everything was all right, Hike and Poodle got a massage and three hours' sleep, and then, with Major Tomkins respectfully sitting in the forward passenger-seat, they went whirling westward again.

General Thorne was saying to himself, "The only thing that I'm sorry for is that I didn't have a chance to give those two boys a banquet. And now let me look into the record of our too-clever Captain Willoughby Welch. I think I see trouble ahead for him!"

CHAPTER X

THAT MILLION DOLLARS

HIKE had scarcely gone a hundred miles before he found that he was going to be too tired to send the *Hustle* as fast as he should; and he immediately started teaching Major Tomkins the principles of driving it. The Major knew nearly every make of aeroplane, and had made a brilliant record, in a Nieuport monoplane, in a St. Petersburg to Turin international race. He soon picked up the few necessary differences in running the *Hustle*; and when they struck the broad plains of the Middle West, Hike finally had a chance to go into that Land of Sleep, into which Poodle had chubbily toddled long since.

Hike awoke once. The machine was stopped; and landed near a Kentucky village. The Major had found that one of the wheels on the chassis was threatening to jar loose, at their terrific speed, and was fixing it. Then Hike peacefully slumbered off again, and did not take the levers till they were over Western Kansas.

* * * *

At Benicia Arsenal, California, they found the Lieutenant, "good old Jack Adeler," as Hike yelled at him, nervously and joyously waiting them. The commandant of the Arsenal insisted on their stopping for dinner, and even Major Tomkins was not treated with greater respect than was young Hike Griffin, whom the commandant toasted admiringly.

Off they whirled to Monterey, and found Martin Priest.

The Associated Press had gathered what news it could about the flight of the *Hustle*, and sent it to newspapers all over the country. The reporters had been told by General Thorne himself that two boys had made the greatest flight in the history of aviation, and that the General was interested in their machine.

That was enough for Martin Priest, and he was sitting at the door of his aerodrome in the sun, smiling to himself, when Major Tomkins, Poodle and Hike found him. He was very happy—but he absolutely refused to appear before the Army Board of Aviation.

"I've lost all my glad-rags and Four-Hundred Manners," he said, rather roughly, to the Major, "and my machine—and Lieutenant Adeler and Hike, here—well, I'm afraid they'll have to speak for me." He said nothing more but there was some one else who had something to say.

Major James Griffin, Hike's father, had become almost chummy with Martin Priest in the last two days, since he learned that Hike had started for Washington. He had been frightened, at first, then a little angry at Hike. But as he learned from Martin Priest how gallantly Hike had been guiding the tetrahedral in flights to San Francisco, and while rescuing the crew of the wrecked yacht, he grew proud and happy. Finally, when the short newspaper reports of the success of the flight began to come in, and to be eagerly discussed with Martin Priest, the Major had chuckled, "Jerry—I was just such a boy—you couldn't have kept me out of West Point! Good boy, Jerry is."

Now, with Hike here before him, tired but successful, and with Major Tomkins bearing a message from General Thorne, to the effect that "that's a great boy of yours, Jim Griffin,"—and with Major Tomkins singing the praises of Hike's manner of driving the *Hustle*—why, all Major Griffin could do was to pound his son affectionately on the back and say, "Go ahead—and don't break your neck, if it's convenient. As for you, young Darby, I suppose I'll get Hail Columbia from your father for letting you go off with this crazy son of mine—but what can I do?"

About that time, the *Hustle's* crew had climbed aboard, with Lieutenant Adeler at the levers, and they were ready to plunge eastward.

Lieutenant Jack Adeler stood before the Army Board of Aviation giving a crisp short account of the Martin Priest Tetrahedral Aeroplane, how it was made, how run, how much it cost, how fast and how slow it could go, how much freight and how many passengers it could carry; and proving the fact that it was the only absolutely safe aeroplane. When he finished, he could not help glancing over at the corner where Captain Willoughby Welch sat, silent and angry.

General Thorne, thanking Lieutenant Adeler for his report—made without notes—ended by following Jack Adeler's glance over at Welch's corner, and said, very dryly:

"As for the eloquent report on the admirable aeroplanes of Messrs. P. J. Jolls and Company, made by Captain Welch, I think that can be forgotten. I wish, of course, in no way to appear to attempt to control the decision of this Board, but, in my opinion, there is no *possibility* of this Board's deciding to devote its funds of nearly a million to the purchase of anything but Priest tetrahedrals—unless it be, perhaps, that some small part of it be devoted to the purchase of one or two machines of one or two other models, for experiment.

"If the persons not members of this Board will now be so kind as to retire, this Board will go into Executive Session.

51

"As for you, Captain Welch, as for *you*—

"But pray pardon me, gentlemen, this is no time and place to take up a matter of discipline.

"Uh, before Mr. Gerald Griffin and Mr. Torrington Darby retire, will some member of this Board offer a suggestion as to a suitable manner of thanking them for—"

"Oh, please don't, General," begged Hike, blushing, adding, under his breath, "Aw, *please* cut it out!"

As they retired from the Board room, Hike knew that the General's long words meant they had won; had *won*! that Martin Priest would have all the money he needed behind him, and no longer be hid from the world by Captain Welch.

But there were other things Captain Welch *could* do.

CHAPTER XI

THE MERRY BELL-BOY

TWO boys lay a-bed till the disgracefully late hour of ten, in twin beds, at the New Willard Hotel, Washington. They didn't feel like great aviators, not they; but like lazy youngsters.

Poodle, having waked up first, had Hike in his power, for he had crawled on Hike's chest and was keeping Hike powerless by pitilessly tickling him under the chin.

When Hike was finally sufficiently awake to throw him off, Poodle discreetly barricaded himself behind an armchair, and, brandishing a pillow, shouted, "Come on, base caitiffs, I defy ye.... Say, Hike, let's pretend we're Boy Aviators, and that we've just come from the Pacific Coast in an aeroplane, and that a Brigadier General has been kow-towing to us."

"Gee, cut it out, Poodle, you make me dizzy."

As Hike held up his hands in a prayer for mercy, Poodle let fly the pillow, which—driven as well as the *Hustle* ever had been—took Hike in the face. Hike dived across the armchair. He was busy drawing stars and crosses on Poodle's face with a lead pencil, while Poodle was dexterously kicking him, when there was a knock.

The knocker was a grinning bell-boy, about Hike's age and build, who seemed much delighted to see the hotel's most famous guests in much disarrayed pajamas, and acting (almost!) as though they were—well, were boys!

"Say, there's a reporter guy downstairs that wants to interview youse. He's a fresh un—I know him. He t'inks he's a winner 'cause he can put down on a paper wot a guy ain't said and draw him like he don't look, both to once."

"Oh, gee, I don't want to get interviewed," wailed Hike. "Say, can't he interview Darby, here? Gwan, Pood', please tell him I've got combobulus of the elevating planes, and my chassis is awf'ly rheumatic and generally Mr. G. J. H. Griffin begs will he please beat it."

"Aw, Hike, I don't want to get interviewed, neither," blushed Poodle, pulling a magnificent new purple dressing-gown about him, and making signs of a desire to jump out of the windows.

"Say, Dr. Bell-Boy, why don't you have him interview you, instead?" requested Hike.

The bell-boy grinned, "Oh, youse guys just wait. There'll be a million and a half reporters here, right away. Associated Press and United Press and all the Washington papers and all the guys wot writes up what they t'ink Congress oughta be doin', for the Kalamazoo Avalanche and the South Sauk Centre Hoop-la. Oh, dere'll be a hot time for youse!"

"Oh, let me die," mourned Hike, and stood on his head on a pillow, as though he were trying to choke himself.

"Say, SAY!" suggested the great Poodle, excitedly, "that's a peach of an idea of yours, Hike. Why not have the reporter chap interview Dr. Bell-Boy for you? Say, Doctor, you said you knew this reporter, but does he know you?"

"Naw. Dat's where a bell-hop gets next. He keeps behind the keyhole and never says nawthin' to nobody no time, and knows everything dat's going on."

"Say," urged Poodle, "you strip off your clothes, and put on Hike's pajamas, and get *in* bed, and let Hike sneak *under* the bed here, and we'll have one splendiferous time with Mr. Reporter, Esquire."

Grinning, the bell-boy obeyed, and while Hike crawled under his bed, with a pillow and a cup of cocoa, the bell-boy became a very sleepy but rather dignified young aviator. Another boy admitted the clever young reporter. Poodle sat by the window, magnificent in his dressing-gown, and listened.

The reporter was a young, young man. He stumbled into the room in a way that made Poodle remark to himself that he "sort of pushed his eye-glasses ahead of him as though he was going to grab something with 'em, and smole real nice—only he just kept that smile for interviews and slapped it on like a hair-puff."

Bowing to Poodle, the reporter said, "Is this Mr. Griffin?"

Poodle shrugged his shoulders, pointed to the bed where the bell-boy lay, and turned back to look out of the window, with great dignity. (This last was spoiled, dreadfully, for Hike found a carpet-tack that was wandering around idly beneath the bed, and shied it out at Poodle, who squeaked and then looked silently foolish.)

Began the reporter: "*Good* morning, Mr. Griffin. I wished—You saw my account of your second flight, in this morning's *Crier*, I hope."

"Yuh. I seen it," growled the bell-boy. "And I been wanting to tell you how it was wrong what you put in the paper. You said how the tehedrum was invented by Bell, the guy what made the telephone, first, and then Priest, he took it up. That ain't right. *I* made it up, outa my own head."

"You did?" feverishly inquired the reporter, writing a couple of words on one sheet of paper, and beginning to sketch the bell-boy on another sheet.

"Sure did I. I told Priest how to make it. You don't believe me, heh? Say, you young slab-sided, four-eyed, grinning, big-toothed, yellow-fingered lump of mud, don't you t'ink that Priest guy'd 'a' brought his blooming old tehedrum hisself, if he—"

"Uh, 'tetrahedral,' you mean, of course, Mr. Griffin," smiled the reporter, *very* politely.

"Aw, you pen-pushers gimme a pain in de apoplexy! 'Tehedrum'—dat's wot all us aviators calls it, see? you bunch o' grins."

"Ahem!" gently protested Poodle, by the window.

"Cheese it!" gently murmured Hike, under the bed, trying to kick the bell-boy through the mattress, without being seen.

"Huk kuh!" gently coughed the reporter, then smiled again. "Your language is very interesting, Mr. Griffin—quite racy. Oh, please don't think I don't *admire* it. I was just contrasting it with the weak-kneed way in which most boys—uh, most young men of your age talk."

"Say, youse. 'F youse don't like de way me talk-trap works, youse kin put a' egg in your shoe and beat it, see? Tell you how it was. You see, me dad—he's a Colonel, his antcisters was dukes and t'ings in England—he didn't want me to grow up like a collidge professor or any o' them softies, so he makes me work in a mine, an' I was to sea, as a cabin-boy (I was wrecked, twict, and I fit with Chink pirates—one of 'em gives me a blob on the head, like to kill me), and I've bummed it—reg'lar hobo, and I was a newsboy in N' Yawk, and a bell-hop in Denver (I licked two *reporters* dere, one time; one of 'em looked an awful lot like you; Smith, his name was; gee! how I did slam dat guy!), and I worked in a machine-shop, carrying left-hand monkey-wrenches to the straw-boss—dat's where I learned about machines."

"Well, well," delightedly chuckled the reporter, making notes of these remarkable adventures. "Splendid story," he was thinking, "splendid." He was very respectful. He was ready to believe almost anything about the boy who had made the greatest aeroplane-flight in history.

"After dat, you kin bet I wasn't no mollycoddle. I could aviate without gettin' cold feet. Me dad, he was a wise guy, all right. Now what else d' yuh want to know?"

"I'd like to know your plans for the immediate future, Mr. Griffin. Will you be making any more aeroplane exhibitions?—With the, uh, the, uh—"

"Don't let it choke you. Be an orful shame to lose a smart young feller like you."

"You know what I mean. Oh, of course—the tehedrum?"

"Say, you willy-boy, wot d' yuh t'ink? T'ink I'm going to rent you me plans, furnished? I'm going to do wot I'm going to do, that's what, see? That SWAT! Ketch the idee? You'd be a smart young man if your feet'd track. Just put that down in your paper, will yuh?" Peeking from under the bed, Hike saw the reporter rise, looking very angry. But the bell-boy was continuing, "And be sure and spell me name right—with a 'x,' y'know. Say, I don' mind telling you I'm thinking of setting me tehedrum to fighting with a battleship."

As the reporter prepared for a crushing reply, the real Mr. Hike Griffin, somewhat dusty, but highly dignified in his bath robe, crawled from under the bed, and said, "Say, I'm awf'ly sorry I let this joke go so far. I'm Griffin. This is a hotel bell-boy. I felt tired, and didn't want to talk, and I thought maybe— Anyway, I apologize. I'll see if I can give you a real interview if you'll wait for me down in the lobby—I'll see about it after breakfast. Really, I'm awf'ly sorry, old man."

"Oh, *that's* all right," said the reporter, in his most sprightly manner, much relieved to find the real Griffin was not so terrible. "I shall be glad to wait in the lobby."

He departed, with young Hike bowing a most courteous and gracious farewell. As the door closed, Poodle looked up from a chair by the window, looked at the bell-boy, grinning on the bed, then at Hike, then began slowly to smile. Hike, at first rather angry, tried to keep sober, then suddenly the three of them were rolling on the bed, kicking and shrieking with joy, till finally Hike gasped:

"Mr. Torrington Darby, we are vulgar."

"Mr. Gerald Griffin, we *are* vulgar!" Poodle solemnly assured him; while, as for the bell-boy, he merely stated:

"Chee! I t'ought I'd die!"

Hike and Poodle had breakfast in their room. As they were fondly contemplating the last crumbs of the toasted-rolls-with-marmalade (lots of marmalade!) the bell-boy returned, to announce, "Say, there's about thirty reporters waiting to talk t' youse, downstairs."

"Well, we'll have to face 'em," said Poodle, bravely.

Hike agreed, and they started down in the elevator. But as Hike stepped out into the lobby, and saw the eager crowd of newspapermen, the courage of the boy who had dared two hundred miles an hour, and armed moonshiners, quite disappeared. Dragging Poodle after him, Hike darted into another elevator, which was just going up. The grill closed in the face of the reporters, who followed the boys up in a third cage, only to find Hike's door locked, and no attention paid to knocks.

Within, Hike was grunting, in reply to Poodle's suggestions that he might as well get the job of being interviewed over, "Aw, I don't want to, Pood'. I ain't done anything—just flown the *Hustle*, and it minds like a pet cat, anyway. It'd make me feel awf'ly foolish to read about what I've done—and what I haven't. The fellows at school'll kid us enough anyway—"

"Gee, they sure will. We'll look like the man that invented butting-in, to them Dignified Seniors. They always think it's fresh for a Sophomore to do anything."

"There you are, you see. And if they read anything we've said to *reporters* in the papers, they'll never let us rest. I ain't afraid of rushing the speed limit, but I don't want the whole San Dinero football team grinning at me like a bunch of hyenas, next Thanksgiving."

"I s'pose you think you'll be the whole School Team, next fall," complained Poodle.

Hike continued, "Say, I've got a good idea. Why can't we escape 'em in the tetrahedral; have Jack Adeler bring it around; and then hang out in some place where the reporters won't find us—say some place in the suburbs— till it's time to go back home in the *Hustle* with Jack."

Hike rushed to the telephone, and, after some moments, got Lieutenant Adeler, though meanwhile the exchange boy downstairs was breaking in with the news that a number of reporters wished to speak with Mr. Griffin on the telephone. Jack Adeler promised to bring the tetrahedral around.

When the Lieutenant sailed slowly over the New Willard, the boys were waiting on the roof. Catching the mounting chains, they climbed up to the *Hustle*, safe from interviews for a while.

It would be a couple of days before the Army Board of Aviation decided just what it wanted to do—whether or not they wanted to spend all of their appropriation on Priest Tetrahedrals. For that time, the Lieutenant arranged that the boys were to stay at the house of a family friend, out in Georgetown,—a suburb of Washington.

* * * *

Lieutenant Adeler and Poodle were walking out to Poodle's new residence, that evening. Hike had gone home earlier, after a day's sightseeing.

The Lieutenant noticed a quiet, strongly built man, with a slouch hat pulled low, following them out P street, but made nothing of it, taking the man for a reporter. But as he and Poodle crossed the Rock Creek bridge, the man ran up at them.

Poodle dropped behind. Out from a shabby house across the bridge two tough-looking negroes dashed. One of them held a revolver at the Lieutenant's head, while the other sprang after Poodle.

Poodle sprang to the rail of the bridge and dropped down into the Rock Creek gully. As he did so, the man who had been following them fired down into the gully, twice.

Poodle crawled into weeds at the side of the creek. He hastened along on hands and knees. Dashing up from the hollow, he ran down Florida Avenue, looking for a policeman.

He found one peacefully strolling along his post, swinging his night-stick.

"Hold-up—army lieutenant held up—bridge!" Poodle gasped, pointing; and followed the policeman who, with drawn revolver, started running.

They found the Lieutenant seated on the rail, swinging his feet calmly and waiting.

"Hullo," he sang out cheerfully. "Get away!"

"Robbed, sir!" bawled the policeman.

"Nope—think they took me for somebody else. They searched me and looked over my letters, but they left my watch and money alone. Looking for papers of some kind, I guess."

By the policeman's request, Poodle and the Lieutenant described the men, as well as they could, at a police station, and strolled on toward Hike's place. Poodle felt distinctly nervous, and this was not at all lessened when, on reaching Hike's room, he found that youngster absent.

They waited for ten minutes, then made inquiries of the Lieutenant's friend who was the boys' host.

"Why," said the owner of the house, "General Thorne sent a carriage for young Mr. Griffin, about an hour ago. Mr. Griffin told me so. And he got in and was driven off."

The Lieutenant was satisfied with that, but Poodle was uneasy. He believed that Hike would have sent him word if he were going away for quite a time. Finally, he persuaded the Lieutenant to telephone.

General Thorne, on the 'phone, said that he had not seen Hike since that noon—when the three of them had lunched with him. "Why, no. Surely not," said the General. He had not sent a carriage for Hike. He had not sent for him at all. He had no idea where he was.

Jack Adeler turned from the telephone to Poodle.

"And those men that held us up seemed to be after papers," was all he said.

Half that night they spent in telephoning, and in searching about the shed where the *Hustle* had been taken. But even at dawn, they found no trace of where Hike was, or of where he had been since he left the house in the carriage that had *not* been sent by the General.

CHAPTER XII

THE LONE CABIN

IN the afternoon before, Hike had been reading in the Washington papers all the things he *hadn't* said to the reporters, and a great many things he hadn't done, with some things such as discovering Crocker Land by aeroplane, which he'd like to do but didn't expect to. His hostess's maid, a colored girl, knocked at his door to say that "a man from Gennul Tho'ne wanted to see him." Going down, Hike found a thick-set, low-browed fellow, built for rough and tumble fights, quietly dressed in neat clothes, who said:

"Mr. Griffin? General Thorne's compliments and he wishes to see you at his office in regard to the aeroplane. He is waiting there—though it's after hours—and would be grateful if you could come at once. I'm connected with the office, and I'll go down with you in the carriage, if you don't mind."

"Certainly. Just a moment, till I get my cap," and Hike dashed upstairs.

He was so busy wondering what General Thorne wanted, and thinking how different it was to ride in a carriage instead of in a gale-tossed aeroplane, that he did not waste much time in asking himself why General Thorne should have sent an ordinary public four-wheeler, with a seedy coachman, instead of a private carriage, or an army Q. M. D. carriage. He noticed that the carriage did not turn directly down toward town, but that did not interest him much till suddenly there they were, emerging on a bridge that certainly was not the Rock Creek Bridge. No—it was the long Aqueduct Bridge, crossing the Potomac—and not leading down town, but to Virginia and the country.

He was surprised and a little indignant. He was starting to ask his companion why they were going this way.

The carriage stopped, the door swung open, another man sprang in and handed to the "messenger from General Thorne" a big cloak, which the latter deftly threw over Hike's head.

Stiffening his lean, sinewy legs, Hike hit out with tangled fists and elbows. He was stifling and his head was all in darkness, but he made out that he had caught his stocky companion a good one in the chest. But strong hands were holding his ankles; others were binding the cloak about him with light rope; then some one was tying his thighs, his ankles, and jerking the cloak ever tighter about him.

To save his strength, Hike sat quite still. He panted with the little air that crept in among the tight folds of the cloak; and the hastily arranged cords seemed to cut his legs in two. But he made himself be calm and think this all out.

Now, he noticed, the cab door had slammed again; and the vehicle had started up. He could feel the vibration of the carriage as the horse's hoofs sharply clattered on the bridge-planks. Apparently the second man, who had brought the cloak, was gone.

"Yump, sure's got something to do with a plot against Priest and the *Hustle*," Hike continued in his thinking. "Well, there's nothing to do but wait. Maybe I'll get a chance at a shindy, bimeby, if I act peaceful, and make 'em think I'm scared. Oh, and a peach of a shindy it'll be if I get the chance to bash the fat head of the kind gentleman that put this muffler on me. And if Cap'n Wibbelty-Wobbelty has anything to do with this—and I've got a funny hunch he has—I hope I'm in at his finish. You bet. 'Fact, I hope I *am* his finish. I remember Dad used to say the Cap'n had 'finished manners.' They'll sure be finished if he's had anything—if he's—he will—"

Hike Griffin was going to sleep!

In those few days of terrific strain in driving the *Hustle*, he had learned that there was nothing that was quite so useless as worrying. Even when things were not going well, it was up to him to wait till he could get the *Hustle* into a calmer current of air.

Well, all right then, he'd have to wait; and rest his nerves till the time when there was something he could do. So now he let himself go to sleep— which he did the more quickly in the close air of the folds of the cloak.

He woke once, to wonder if any policeman had noticed the curious stopping of the four-wheeler on the Aqueduct Bridge. He had a funny little picture of Poodle, dressed as a policeman, riding an aerial motorcycle, stopping the *Hustle* for speeding, and then changing into a general and conducting a large brass band. This last sound was caused by the ringing in his ears.... He seemed to be choking.... He tried to pull at the cloak.

Then, some one was loosening it a little, so that he could breathe. He fell asleep again.

Once more he awoke. He was being carried out of the four-wheeler, and, apparently, placed in a wagon, and covered with something that smelled as though it might be hay. Then this wagon—if that was what it was—went jolting off. He heard it dully, drowsily.

After what may have been any number of hours, Hike really woke up. The cloak had been removed from his eyes. It was now night. He was lying in front of a door, dimly seen by a small lantern; a rough door of unpainted pine. Judging from the way he could look down and see starry sky, he was on a hill.

Though he still kept his nerve, Hike had never been so confused in his life as he was then. Where was he? Why had he been taken there? Who were his captors? What did they want? A thousand questions were pounding away inside his sorely aching head, even while he drew in deep delightful breaths of fresh air.

Gradually he made out something of the place. The door belonged to a log cabin, apparently not twenty-five feet long. There was a rough doorstone—simply a flat rock; up to which led a rude path overgrown with struggling grass. The roof was of thatch, or of thatch and boards. He couldn't make out, in that dim light. Overhead was the good clean sweep of star-lit heavens. (If he were only up there, in the *Hustle!*) Trees rustled near him. The hill seemed well-wooded.

Far away, seemingly, there was the bound of a wagon—that must be, he thought, the vehicle in which he had been brought. Frogs were loudly piping down at the foot of the hill. (Must be marshes there, he thought. Marshes—if he had to escape, he'd remember that.)

But what of the men who had brought him? Well, that was what he was wondering. Then he heard noises within the cabin, a light was kindled, and he made out a broken window, near the door. At the door appeared the stocky man who, "coming from General Thorne," had enticed him away. The fellow was now clad in sweater, cap, and laced leather hoots. He bore a rifle. All his business-like, suave expression had changed to a hard, criminal look.

Behind him was a taller thug with a vicious twist to his mouth, leering at Hike. This taller person said to Hike's first captor, "Well, Bat, you watch for a couple of hours and then call me, and I'll get on the job, heh?"

"Yup. All right," said Bat, as the two men stooped and lifted Hike. They bore him into the cabin, and dropped him roughly on the floor.

"Now I guess you'll run tetrahedrals—*not*, young smart Aleck," snarled the taller man.

"Shut up, Snafflin. Beat it," ordered Bat.

"A' right. Keep your collar on. Got the makings?"

Bat scowled at the vicious companion, and silently handed him cigarette papers and tobacco. While the taller tough rolled a cigarette, Hike, watching the lean, quick, yellow-stained fingers, sympathized with his enemy Bat for having to play with tall Mr. Snafflin, who was the sort of chap to make a good pick-pocket, or a better sneak-thief, with those quick, hideous fingers.

"Well," and Snafflin stretched, scratched his head and yawned, "well, guess I'll pound my ear. How do you feel, youngster? You ain't saying much, are you? Sorry—'cause if you said anything I'd smash your jaw, and that'd tickle me, all right, all right."

Just then, Bat the stocky turned his back. The tall rascal deliberately kicked Hike in the chest, strolled to the door, and disappeared.

Then Bat came back, bringing a rolled coat which he thrust under Hike's head.

"Griffin," he said quietly, "I'm sorry we had to kidnap you. I can't tell you why, but you'll find out. You won't be badly treated. I'll see you get enough to eat—that is, if you listen to reason, to-morrow or next day, when a gentleman comes to talk to you about a little matter.... I guess you're wise to what's up—something to do with that fool aeroplane. But I don't know what it is, and I don't want to.... Well, you're a brave kid, all right; and I never knew one that could keep his mouth shut as well as you can.... Good night."

Then Hike spoke his first words since he had been captured. "Good night. Much obliged for the pillow." He twisted his head around, and pretended to go to sleep.

But he didn't. One reason why he had made himself go to sleep when covered by the cloak—even after it had been loosened enough to give him tolerable air to breathe—was so that when the time came he could stay awake. And that time was now.

Through narrowed eyelids, he saw Bat roam to the door, and sit on the sill, lazily looking out, his rifle resting against his knees.

The room, Hike made out, could not have been used for years. It had evidently been the home of the poorest sort of "poor white trash" farmers. The floor was littered with broken whiskey-bottles and dirt. In the wretched light, given by a small lantern placed on a rickety wooden table by the wall, Hike could see that weeds had thrust themselves up through the cracks of the puncheon-floor. In one corner was piled broken furniture—a couple of wretched wooden chairs, the wreck of a bed, a few broken dishes.

The light, flickering, made ghostly shadows along the thatch. In all, it was far more desolate than a haunted ruin.

Hike did not spend very much time thinking about that, however. He had to plan an escape.

His knife and what little money he had on his person had been taken by the tall Snafflin. How could he cut the two bonds, of thin but strong and new rope, which fastened his wrists and ankles?

He wriggled away at them, making as little motion as possible, and saw that it would be impossible to untie them. The knots were tight. Then he would have to burn them—yes, and he'd do it, though he did not carry a single match. He had something better—nitric acid!

Martin Priest had always been interested in chemical experiments, to find the best explosive for use with bombs to be dropped from aeroplanes; one lighter and safer than any other. Hike had worked with him, at Monterey, making tiny mixtures of strong chemicals, and he had a little case of chemicals, that was still with him. In it was a small vial of strong nitric acid—which eats through rope, rotting it; and which turns the fingers strangely orange.

He made loud noises of sleepiness, deliberately getting Bat to look at him, from the door. He curled up, as though for more comfortable slumber. As he twisted about awkwardly, easing the strain of the bonds, he caught the case of chemicals from his pocket, pulled out the nitric acid bottle, shoved the case under him. When he finally lay still, his bound ankles were near the hand that was tightly closed over the vial.

Very cautiously, not moving an inch a minute, he drew out the stopper of the little bottle, and let the liquid drop on the bonds between his hands; then on the rope between his ankles. He took every care to keep the acid from falling on his flesh and his clothes. The task was a strain. He had to clamp his jaws together. But he kept at it.

Now, all he had to do was to wait, and the rope would soon be so rotted that a slight pull would separate ankle from ankle, and wrist from wrist. He waited.

The spot in his chest where tall Snafflin had kicked him was aching. That gave him an idea. No; he wouldn't attack Bat. Bat wasn't so bad, even if he had first enticed him away. He would wait, till the other took his turn as guard, and then try to make it interesting for him.

He did not worry; he held himself in. He heard Bat call, "Hey you, Pete Snafflin. Wake up. Two o'clock. Get up, will you? Your turn on guard."

So then, reflected Hike, the name of the tall and vicious rascal was Mr. Peter Snafflin, and the time was two of the morning. Well, that didn't make much difference to him! He'd just as soon bash the head of Mr. Snafflin if his name were O'Flannagan or Moskowski or Li Hung Chang; and as soon do it at noon as at two A. M.

So he kept on talking to himself. Poodle had taught him that trick of holding cheerful conversations with himself; and he kept at it only the more because he wanted to be calm while he waited to find out what his new guard would do.

Bat went out, Snafflin strolled in, rolling another of his cigarettes. The lantern cast his lean cruel shadow on the rough walls. He came up, deliberately stooped and slapped Hike's cheek. Hike pretended to awake with a start, then—while Snafflin watched him—to groan, and turn over a bit to sleep again. As he turned over, he felt the rotted bonds give a little.

Snafflin wandered to the doorstep, rolled up a coat, and lay stretched out into the darkness. Then he swore viciously (Hike watching him all the while, oh, so closely!) and, for greater comfort, stuck his coat-pillow on the ground just in front of the door. His rifle was left carelessly beside him.

Was it possible, Hike wondered, that the man had gone to sleep on guard? Mr. Snafflin looked like too capable a tough to do that. Hike made himself keep quiet till he saw, by the faint glow from Snafflin's cigarette-end, that Snafflin, though lying so sprawled out, was wide awake, out there on the dark doorstep.

So then, Hike couldn't rush out. Glancing about the shack, he made out the window beside the door. All its glass was broken; half its frame gone.

If he could get over to that window and drop out something on the peaceful Snafflin—!

He noticed a long bed-slat in the heap of broken furniture. That would do the trick.

He gave a quick though quiet jerk. His wrist bonds strained, then the acid-rotted cord pulled apart, strand by strand. His hands were free, though the cord still clung obstinately about his left wrist. Then he broke the rope between his ankles. But he still lay there, till after Snafflin had taken another lazy glance into the cabin, and had settled down still more comfortably.

Then Hike made a quick, low-bent, silent dive, and caught the bed-slat out of the pile of furniture. He sprang to the window. He thrust out the slat. Snafflin's rifle lay near the window, outside the shack. Hike poked the end of the slat underneath, lifted the rifle, and hurled it away. It clattered down on a rock, fifteen feet away. The surprised guard sat up, with a jerk.

Hike brought the slat down, hard, on the head of Snafflin, who fell back on the door-stone. Hike ran to the door, leaped out over Snafflin, and darted away from the cabin. Behind him, he heard the man's shrill, ugly voice, whimpering loudly, "Bat! Bat! He's got away!"

Hike was almost instantly in the darkness, confused by bushes and pools of water. He fell flat over a broken bough, on the earth. He was all confused, as he scrambled up. His legs were both stiff and weak. They wanted to give way. But he made them go, and plunged down hill, through the underbrush, toward the marsh where he could again hear the frogs.

If he could gain that, he could at least make it hard for the two men to catch him. He heard them raging, cursing, running, behind him.

He crossed a bog, and suddenly he was ankle-deep in mud, while the mosquitoes sang about him in crowds. He tested the mud carefully and kept going, onward, into the marsh, though the mud grew deeper, and presently he had to cling to the branches of what seemed, in the utter darkness, to be stunted oaks, to keep from sinking in.

Hike had swiftly decided that the one thing the men would *not* expect a youngster to do was keep on going into a marsh. They would be sure to think that he would either reach the road, or stay on the edge of the marsh.

He quietly broke off tree branches, and made of them a safe matting which would not let him sink into the mud. Then he wrapped his coat about his head, to keep off the scourge of mosquitoes, and pulled his trouser cuffs down to his shoe tops, to protect his ankles. Even so, the pests tormented him. But he kept very still, peering out of a tiny opening at the coat collar, which he had left for his eyes.

He saw lanterns darting about the hill top. One came down, apparently carried by a man who was following the road. There was the sound of a horse's neighing, some distance away, and then Hike had the worst shock of the night.

From some distance away, along the road clattered three or four horses' hoofs; and the shouts of three or four riders were heard. So, then, the two thugs had companions, who had been sleeping over there, somewhere in the great darkness which was making him feel so "awf'ly alone" against all these men.

The horsemen were circling, quartering what seemed to be fields about the hill; hunting over every inch of the hill itself. At last, he saw the lanterns, which marked the searchers, draw together, at the edge of the marsh, and he heard a loud voice:

"Well, I tell you he must be in the marsh—way in, then, Bat. We've looked everywhere else. He couldn't 've gotten far."

"All right," came Bat's voice. "Get out that auto light, then, and we'll search the blooming marsh."

A horseman galloped away, soon returning. Then, to his horror, Hike saw the group at the edge of the marsh kindle what looked to be a powerful head-light, with strong reflectors. Its rays swept through the thickets of the marsh, as the light was slowly turned.

A shout sounded from the knot of horsemen as the beams struck Hike. He knew that he was found.

Calmly rising, he drew on his coat, stooped to kill a mosquito that had caught in a fold, and strolled out through the thick mud as calmly as though he were walking through the Santa Benicia Academy Yard.

The men on the edge of the marsh received him with a broad grin.

"Well," said Hike to them, "I think I'll go to bed. Tired of walking. Say, have you got anything to eat?"

"Kid," said Bat, the leader, "you're all right. (Shut up, you Snafflin—you only got what was coming to you!)"

"Mosquitoes kind of thick to-night," observed Hike, cheerfully. "Think we'll have a little rain. Seems wet." He stooped down and brushed an imaginary speck of dust off the only place on his trousers that was not thick with mud.

"You're all right," grinned Bat, again. "Hanged if I'm going to tie you up again. But there'll be two men—*two*—watching you, all the time. Kid for a kid—yes, and for a man—you're a wonder. Say, how did you cut through them ropes without a knife?"

"I let your friend Snafflin look at 'em," said Hike, "and they just rotted in two. Well, I guess I'll go to bed. Is the water hot enough for a bath?"

CHAPTER XIII

DETECTIVE POODLE

LIEUTENANT ADELER and Poodle Darby had not received a single word from Hike, even by noon of the day after his disappearance.

General Thorne grew alarmed. The police were quietly notified, without letting the newspapers know; and two police detectives were put on the case. Besides them, two operatives from a good private detective-agency were employed. The great Poodle had to box his own ears, to keep from feeling conceited at the way in which these private detectives consulted him; and the anxious respect with which they hinted that they knew how Poodle had aviated with Hike across the country.

Poodle talked the case over with Lieutenant Adeler; suggesting that Captain Willoughby Welch must have something to do with the matter; but this the Lieutenant, good army-man as he was, refused to listen to. Then Master Poodle took a long walk with himself, and thought the whole thing over thoroughly. He decided: "Here's where I become a grand little detective."

He felt very certain that Mr. P. J. Jolls and Captain Welch knew a great deal about the matter. He found, by telephoning, that Captain Welch, who was staying at the New Willard, had been seen loafing about the lobby, talking to acquaintances and reporters, all day. That, Poodle decided, was for the sake of appearances. Captain Welch was not, he believed, so clumsy a rascal that he needed to be doing mischief himself, in order to get it done; and, anyway, it was good Mr. Jolls who was likely to be causing the real trouble.

Where was Mr. Jolls? He was supposed to be in Chicago. There his factories were located. But suppose he were in Washington? His name had not been mentioned in the newspapers; he had not been seen about the State, War, and Navy Building, where the Board of Aviation had been holding its meetings. But Poodle felt sure that the man was here; that his fat hand had something to do with the disappearance of Hike.

He described Jolls to one of the private detectives. He had seen the airship magnate at Captain Welch's house, in Monterey. He mentioned Jolls' sausage-roll neck, his red little eyes, the four gaudy rings he wore.

The detective started his search, without confiding in any one except Poodle. He searched through several of the larger hotels.

Poodle waited in the anteroom of General Thorne's office.

There was a telephone call for him. Over the wire, he heard the detective reporting, "Hullo. Darby? Well, there's a guy here at the Hotel de Suisse that—"

"Hotel de Suisse?"

"Yuh, it's a small hotel but very swell—lot of rich people that are here lobbying use it. Well, there's a guy here named Jolls. He ain't registered. But I got wise to him through a bell-hop. And he looks just like you said the right Jolls did."

"A' right. Be right there. Meet me in lobby. Say, just kill Jolls for me, while you're waiting, will you?" exclaimed Poodle, and, jamming the receiver on the hook, dashed out of the telephone booth.

"Call me a taxi!" he shrieked at an orderly. The soldier jumped to obey. Poodle waited for the taxi on the walk, and swung into it before it had stopped.

"Hotel de Suisse—quick—big tip if you hustle!" he hissed at the chauffeur, slammed the door to himself, and was off.

Though he had just been the busy detective, it was the real Poodle that curled up on the cushions in a most undignified way, and poked fun at himself for the way he had been ordering people about. And he grinned. "Gee, I sure am glad Papa Darby is rich—but I don't know's he will be, for long, if he has to back his little Poodle in this search for Hike." Rejoicing at being able to pay bills at this important time, he clinked the gold coins he had brought from California (where very little paper-money is used).

As the taxi whirled up to the Hotel de Suisse, Poodle jumped out, threw a gold piece to the astonished chauffeur, then sauntered into the hotel as though he were bored to death and wishing he had something to do.

The detective was seated in a big leather armchair in the lobby, looking oh! so lazy and careless. But there was no laziness in his sharp whisper to Poodle:

"Jolls upstairs. In his room. Ain't been out since he came—two, three days ago—but gets lots of 'phone calls. He's ordered an early breakfast for to-morrow—six o'clock; in his room. And a touring car for six-twenty."

"Do you know any of the night-clerks here?" asked Poodle.

"Yuh. Sure. A little. Why?" The detective threw out the four remarks as though they were so many hard rocks.

"Look here. I'll watch here till midnight. Then you watch till morning, and get me up at a quarter to six—I'll get a room here, you know. Will you?"

"Yuh. Sure. Quarter to six."

"And say," added Poodle, "get me a suit of clothes so's I can make up as a kind of a tough kid.... Now you look here—if you say, 'You won't need much disguise for that,'—why, I'll bite you."

"You've got me," grinned the detective. "I was going to make some fool crack like that!"

Poodle hastened out to get a couple of sandwiches and a cup of coffee, engaged a room, and settled down for his six-hour wait till midnight, in the lobby, telephoning his whereabouts to the Lieutenant.

He did not expect to see Mr. P. J. Jolls that evening, but he did—once. The man came down in an elevator, crossed the lobby, bought some papers, and returned to his room. He went quickly, as though he were in hiding. He glanced about the lobby, with an anxious expression in his fat, mean face, but he didn't notice the cheerful youngster who was so deep sunk in the big chair nearest the elevator.

Next morning, at a quarter to six, one Poodle Darby was very busily engaged in sleeping, with his head deeply buried in a pillow. The detective, entering by means of a pass-key, stood by the bed, grinned, then began to tickle Poodle's happy red ears till Poodle awoke and stared up, wondering why and where and what.

"Hawlf awfter steen, me lud, and the bawth waits," announced the detective.

Poodle's first reply was a remarkable combination of a yawn, a stretch, a sigh, and "Gee, I'm sleepy," all of which, taken together, sounded very much like "Ughff—F!" Then he regarded the detective with extreme disfavor and added, "You talk like a little green wagon. Oh, say, has the motor car come yet?"

"No. It ain't due yet. Jolls didn't order it to come till six-twenty."

"I mean the one for me."

"For you? You didn't say anything about that."

"GEE! Did I forget it? I've got to have one—to follow him."

"Yuh. That's what I thought. So I ordered one for you—a touring-car. Now who talks like a little green wagon?" The detective smiled infernally.

While hastily dressing in the rough coat, trousers and shirt of his "disguise," Poodle reflected that he hadn't the best of it, for once. So he loved the detective. Poodle was built that way—he liked people who could do things better than he.

Poodle was in the tonneau of his car, waiting in front of the hotel, when Mr. P. J. Jolls pompously came down and entered a second automobile. Poodle was wilted down in the corner, with a large steamer-rug concealing nearly all of him except an extra large and ferocious pair of goggles, and the tip of his merry upturned nose.

He ordered his chauffeur to follow the Jolls car; and away they hustled, out through old Georgetown, across the Aqueduct Bridge into Virginia, then northeastward, through little towns and past farms, in which Poodle took about as little interest as a sailor would in a horse. For he was attending strictly to this question: did Mr. P. J. Jolls know that his car was being followed?

At first, so many cars were touring that Jolls noticed nothing. But as Poodle's car kept on taking the same turns as he did, even after they had left the highroad, Jolls began to look back, anxiously. Finally, they reached a hilly country, and from hilltops Jolls looked down on the pursuing car anxiously.

They approached a great hill, and Jolls' car slowed down.

Poodle ordered his chauffeur, "Pass that car, and take me just over the top of the hill. I'll jump out there, but you go ahead, and wait for me at the next town. You may have to wait all day."

The chauffeur had been told by the detective that this lad was really a great young sleuth, and there was keen respect in the "Yes, sir" with which he answered Poodle.

They shot by the Jolls car, Poodle keeping way down in the tonneau. As soon as the car passed the top of the hill, where it was hidden from the Jolls car for an instant, Poodle sprang out. He looked like a jolly country-boy, certainly not like a motorist who followed other people's cars. He strolled to the top of the hill, and over it, toward the approaching Jolls car, without attracting the slightest attention from Jolls.

He ambled down till he was just behind the Jolls car, which was taking the hill very slowly. Poodle was sure that Jolls would never go to his real destination, where Hike was, unless he got rid of the car that seemed to be pursuing him. He had been sure that Jolls would slow up, to let the other car get ahead. He chuckled cheerfully to find that he had guessed right.

Once behind the car, the loafing country-boy suddenly changed to a panting runner. Poodle dashed up behind the Jolls car, caught at the back-thrust hood, and swung up beneath it, clinging to the springs and back of the car with his toes. As the car, passing the top of the hill, increased its speed a little, Poodle settled himself, not into a comfortable position, but into a safe one, crouching on the trunk rack. As he had expected, the Jolls car took a side road at the bottom of the decline, to escape the "pursuing car" ahead; then let out speed.

They rode about seven miles, with Poodle swaying behind, then, in a small town they stopped. Poodle dropped from behind, and vaulted upon a fence, looking as rustic as he could.

Mr. P. J. Jolls climbed stiffly out of the car, his fat legs objecting to exercise; and said to Poodle:

"Say, boy, where's Smith's Livery-Stable?"

"I dunno, sir; I don't belong in this here town," Poodle drawled as ignorantly as possible.

Mr. Jolls looked at him with haughty scorn, and trotted down the street. To Jolls' chauffeur Poodle said:

"What's the trouble with you and the old man? What's he dropping you for, and taking to a livery-stable? My, you must be a bum shuffler. If I was driving a man and he ditched me—"

"Ditched nobody," growled the chauffeur. "I'm to wait. I suppose if *you* was chauffeur you'd be so good he just couldn't lose you," Jolls' driver sneered in a highly superior manner.

"You go eat your hat," ordered Poodle, very impudently perhaps, and dropped on the further side of the fence to escape the wrench which the chauffeur was going to throw at him.

He strolled through the little town, and watched Mr. Jolls groaningly hoist himself up on horseback, and ride painfully away.

Then Poodle's loafing manner disappeared. Holding out a gold piece, he said to Smith of Smith's Stables, "Give me your best saddle-horse. Quick. But without a saddle. And I want that big straw-hat, there on the wall."

The proprietor started to quiz him, but Poodle abruptly, curtly, cried, "Quick, I said. This five bucks is for you."

As soon as he was out of the stable-yard, Poodle pulled off his shoes and socks and tucked them under his coat. He pulled his straw-hat down on his head. Then he loped round a corner, and was soon going at a lazy country pace, along the dusty, hot road, behind Mr. P. J. Jolls. He stuck out his bare feet, and slouched all over his horse's back. Jolls took only one look back at him, then paid no further attention.

Poodle rejoiced to see from the way Jolls shifted in his seat that the manufacturer was good and uncomfortable. He needed a little cause for rejoicing like that, for Poodle was not any too comfortable, himself. He had got used to the hard slippery McClellan army-saddles, at Monterey. But this clinging to the sides of a sweating horse, without a saddle, was not pleasant.

He rolled and slid, but he followed closely enough, till Jolls turned in at a private road, which led by a marsh up a wooded hill, where stood a lonely old shack.

Poodle rode by, round a bend, slid off his horse, hitched it back in a thicket, and darted across the road into a field of the abandoned farm which Jolls had entered. He slipped on his shoes and hid the huge straw hat. Running with his head and shoulders low, taking shelter behind shrubs, he approached the hill from behind. Suddenly, his feet sank in mud. A marsh was before him. He ran along its edge, and found that the boggy land surrounded all the hill, except where the road entered, in front.

He jerked off his shoes and rushed into the marsh on the jump. Mud soaked through his socks. Briers scratched him. But he went at the bushes as though they were open doors. He didn't have time to notice he was being scratched and soaked.

He reached the hillside and sneaked up it on hands and knees. For he had been startled by the sight of a tall, vicious-faced man, strolling about the top of the hill, with a rifle under his arm, as though he were guarding the cabin toward which Poodle was heading.

Once he had to lie flat for three minutes, while mosquitoes covered him. But he didn't care. Hike must be up there in the cabin!

The guard passed out of sight. Poodle rushed to the cabin. He found a rubbish heap—old shoes, bottles, a couple of boards, damp straw—at the back of the house, and slipped under this ill-smelling but concealing heap. Putting his ear against a crack in the old logs, he almost cried out with joy, for he heard Hike's voice within. Hike was saying:

"There's no use talking to me, Mr. Jolls. I haven't got anything to say about the Priest aeroplanes. You ought to know that. All I do is to drive them. And if you did anything to me, you'd have just as much trouble."

"Now I *know*, my boy—" came P. J. Jolls' greasy voice, soothingly.

"Now I know," Poodle heard Hike interrupting, in there, in the cabin, "I know that you and Captain Welch are trying to steal Priest's rights from him and get the army-appropriation for your old machines. I'm sorry I haven't got any final say about the thing, because if I did have I'd fight you to the end. But I haven't got the least bit to say. So you're only wasting your time trying to get me to keep away from Priest. Why, can't you see for yourself, I'm only a kid, and—"

"Yes, my boy, I can see you're 'only a kid.' Not so much because of your appearance, but because you won't listen to reason. Now you listen to me." Poodle felt that Mr. Jolls was getting rather angry. "I *know*, from inside sources, the Army Board is going to throw out the Priest aeroplane entirely, because it isn't practical for use in war."

"You're a liar," Hike was heard to state, wearily and most impolitely.

"Will you listen to me, or not?"

"Oh, yes, I suppose I'll have to—tied up like this. And it was you that made 'em tie me again. I won't forget that."

When he heard the words "tied up," Poodle's flesh prickled coldly all over. Hike—*tied up*! He felt that any punishment he could devise for Jolls would be too easy. Well, he'd try to hit Jolls in the pocketbook. That would hurt more than anything else! Meanwhile, Jolls was continuing:

"I wish you could understand me, Griffin. I don't believe I've ever admired any young man so much as I admired you when I heard of the magnificent way in which you handled that rotten Priest tetrahedral in your cross-country flight. Why, I want you to be one of my chief aviators, my boy. At a great big salary. I've met your father—I have the keenest—"

"You let my father alone, will you?" snapped Hike.

"—the keenest admiration for him, and I hate to see his son mixed up with a swindler and fake inventor like Priest. Why, my boy, what few things there are that're good about Priest's tetrahedral are *stolen*! Stolen from other devices that are patented. Mr. Priest will land in jail inside of one week—"

"That's another lie," Hike remarked.

"It is, eh? Well, do you want to go to jail with him? Er no, I've got something better for you. Now listen." Mr. Jolls made his voice to be very soft and purring. "If you'll just sit down and write a little note like this, I'll give you a thousand dollars—in coin. Write like this: 'My *dear* Mr. Priest: I have decided that the tetrahedral is taking up too much of my time, and I shall have to drop it. You can run the thing yourself. Also, I know that you have stolen all your patents, and I don't want anything to do with you, or your thefts, I might add.'

"Now a note like that won't hurt anything—you must see that yourself— if he *hasn't* stolen them; and, if he has, why it will be only just. If the cap fits, let him put it on."

"Sure," Hike could be heard sniffing, "it won't hurt him—merely break his heart—just when he's getting over the feeling that the whole world is conspiring against him. He's pretty fond of me. All that note will do will be to send him out into the mountains again, and probably make him give up the game entirely."

"Oh, don't worry about that," Jolls snarled, the politeness in his nasty voice wearing very thin. "That isn't the only way we're going to get at your precious Priest. There's plenty of other strings that we're pulling, already. Your note won't be more than a drop in the bucket. It won't hurt Priest a quarter so much as some of the other things we're going to do. Don't let that hurt your sweet young conscience. You might just as well take the thousand dollars I'm giving you, and be easy.

"Think, son, just think of the things you can do with that thousand." Jolls' voice was soft again, in there. "Why, you can make aeroplane experiments of your own. See here. I haven't stated the other side, yet. If you *don't* write that note, there'll be two less boys by to-morrow night—not only you, but your young friend Torrington Darby—what is it you call him? Poodle, is it? I won't tell you what will happen to him, except that we have him in a trap, too. But as for you—"

"You make me tired," Hike could be heard yawning, apparently not much impressed.

"I'll make you much tireder before I get through with you if you don't write this note," Jolls roared. "Look here. You ought to know, by this time, after the way you were brought here, and the way you're guarded, that I can do whatever I want to with you. I might as well admit that I won't stop short of anything, to land this contract for aeroplanes. I'm going to have it, and if you think a brat like you can put any hindrances in my way, you might just as well get over that idea right *now*! You might as well take this thousand dollars that I'm simply *giving* you, and be easy.

"And if you *don't* write that note, let me tell you what will happen to you. I'll let you have till to-morrow to make up your mind. If you won't write this note—which I'll telegraph to your dear friend Priest, signed with your name, in any case, whether you write it or not, so you might just as well—"

"Gee, you've got a nice little brain," Hike could be heard laughing. "You just thought of that, didn't you? Why didn't you think of it before? You can go ahead and telegraph, all right—so what's the *use* of my writing the note? Course you were going to send it by mail, with my writing but—"

"Well, the note will be handy for proving *you* sent the wire," Jolls declared. "I want it, that's all you need to know. And if you don't write it, here's what I'll do. I'll have my men dig out a nice little hole in the marshes below here. You know what they're like—my men told me about that fool attempt to escape that you made last night. You may remember that there's one or two mosquitoes there. Well, you will be tied there, and left—without a drop of water to drink. Nothing to eat—your stomach will draw up its sides, you'll feel faint—oh, you'll have a nice time. You'll get weaker and weaker till you can't lift a finger to chase away the mosquitoes. They will cover you!"

In his hiding place, Poodle was raging, but he kept quiet, as Jolls went on:

"And you'll keep sinking—I don't know which'll get you first, mud or starvation or mosquitoes. You'll enjoy it. Just think of last night, and how much you liked the mosquitoes, in the marsh.... Now will you write that note? Or, maybe, do you think I'm just talking to hear myself talk? Do you think that I wouldn't be glad to have you tied up, down there in the marsh?"

Poodle waited with painful eagerness for Hike's answer. Hike had seen what Jolls' men could do—what did he believe—did he think that Jolls would really do this thing, or not? He was so anxious for the answer that he half withdrew himself from the concealing pile of rubbish; then plunged down again, and listened from below the crack in the wall, for he heard the leisurely step of the guard with the rifle.

"Well," Hike could be heard saying, after a pause, "I guess you're just about enough of a skunk to do that. It won't do you any good though. I won't write that note, and that's all there is to it. Besides, a great uncle of mine died in the swamps during the Civil War.... I don't see where I'm any better than he was.... I'm sleepy now. I don't think I'm very anxious to talk to you, any longer."

Poodle heard Hike pretend to snore. Jolls swore. Then the cabin door slammed. Some one yelled, "Come here, you fellows, Mr. Jolls wants to talk to you."

Poodle was frightened. He believed that Hike thought he was going to be killed. Never had he loved and admired Hike so much as he did then.

He crawled near a corner of the shack, and saw a group of five toughs, surrounding Jolls and listening to him. Their voices were not loud. They were talking things that men do not want heard, ever. The droning burr of the locust in the golden haze of noon was louder.

In a few minutes, Jolls stalked off, down the hill, and the thugs took their former places, two of them on guard, the others loafing under the trees, smoking, laughing, carelessly talking.

Poodle wasn't doing any of these three things. He hastened back to his rubbish heap, to get hidden before the guard came 'round back of the cabin.

He pulled the damp straw as far up over him as it would go, and slanted a couple of stray boards over the pile, so that it hid him. Making himself as small as he could, under the rubbish, he picked at the crack at which he had been listening.

The mud-filling between the logs had never been put on very well, and now it was crumbling badly, dry and flaky. He worked at it with his fingers till they bled, then poked it with his little penknife. Gradually, he made a hole clean through. Twisting about, he could look into the cabin.

He was startled, at first, for he was looking right at a guard, who stood in the open doorway, across from him. Then he saw the dirty floor, the broken window, and the heap of old furniture. Finally, he located Hike, lying not over five feet from him, on the floor. Hike's ankles and wrists were tied, and a rope bound about his waist was hitched to a ring in the wall. He looked very tired, but his lean jaw was firmly set. He seemed to be going off to sleep again, instead of worrying.

"*Hike!*" whispered Poodle, after two or three minutes, when the guard for the back and sides of the cabin had passed by, and the guard in front had moved out a little from the door. "Hike! It's Pood'!"

Hike started up, then lay back, with closed eyes. Hadn't he been able to believe his own ears? Did he think he had dreamed that whisper?

But Hike crossed his fingers, twice. It was the sign of the Santa Benicia fraternity to which the two boys belonged! And Poodle was sure that Hike had heard, and was making the signal for him.

"Out back," whispered Poodle, a word at a time, cautiously, peeping out from his rubbish heap now and then, to be sure the guard was not near him. "I'll come in *Hustle*—rescue. When's Jolls coming back?"

Suddenly a strange sound came from within the cabin. Hike was singing, as though to amuse himself. Poodle wondered, as he heard:

"Santa Benicia, Santa Benicia,
Santa Benicia Acada*mee*."

Hadn't Hike heard him, then, after all?

He saw the guard in front look into the cabin, and heard him sneer, "Call that singing? I'd kill my dog, if he howled that way." The guard strolled still farther out from the cabin.

Hike sang on, through two verses, mumbling the words badly. Poodle started, as he made out words among the mumblings. He listened intently, and got this message out of what sounded like nonsense:

"To-night. Meeting here. Heard Jolls. Heard him talking. In front of cabin. Captain Welch will be here. Have him arrested. Come in *Hustle*. God bless you, old Poodle!"

"I'll be here," whispered Poodle. As the guard, passing the back of the cabin, turned the corner, Poodle slipped out of his rubbish heap, and crept toward the nearest bushes.

Running, stumbling, hurrying till his panting heart pained him, he rushed down the hill, toward the marsh, bound for Washington.

CHAPTER XIV

AIR-PILOT POODLE

POODLE had ridden seven miles behind the Jolls automobile, but he had to walk twelve, for it was five miles from the hill where he had left his own car to "the next town," where he had told his chauffeur to wait for him.

Twelve miles of hard, fast walking, while the Virginia August sun made his head ache till every snapping farmhouse dog that ran out seemed like a dragon, and he could scarcely see the glaring fields, smelling of jimson and milkweed. The dust, the endless deep dust of the road, got into his throat and caked on his wet feet and legs. But he never stopped, and found his chauffeur waiting him, well on in the afternoon.

The man grinned at his appearance, but he straightened up and dived out of the car, to crank up, startled at the way in which Poodle yelled, "Back to Washington—your best speed."

Poodle crawled wearily into the tonneau, and tried to scrape off some of the dirt. He had always dressed rather beautifully, but he couldn't help his looks now. He hated to face the General's servants, dirty as he was, but he'd just have to, he decided.

They whirled into town shortly after six, and down M street toward General Thorne's home. A servant somewhat curtly told this roughly dressed country boy that General Thorne was out at dinner. No; he didn't know where.

Poodle had to find the orderly who knew him before he could get the butler to tell him that the General was dining with the military attaché of the British Embassy, at the most gorgeous restaurant in Washington.

Poodle hurried there. He broke through a line consisting of hat-boys, the head waiter, and the cigar-clerk, who tried to keep him out. He rushed up to the General's table.

The lackeys were horrified as they saw the young rustic, with dried mud up to his knees, and bits of old straw still clinging in his tangled hair, hurry to the General. They summoned a special policeman and started after him. But they stopped, amazed. For the General held out his hand, and motioned Poodle to take a seat at the table with him and the English attaché, a handsome gentleman with a monocle—and a surprised stare!

Worried though he was, Poodle had to grin at the excitement now spreading through the whole restaurant. Then he whispered sharply to the General, "Found Hike—prisoner—taken by Jolls. In cabin—way over in Virginia.

Captain Welch and Jolls have meeting there, to-night. Hike—Jerry, I mean —may be killed, for refusing to write a letter to Priest that Jolls wants. Will you take a couple of soldiers and come over there to-night, with Lieutenant Adeler and me, in the tetrahedral—get the goods on Welch?"

"Yes," whispered the General. "Get hold of Adeler, and I'll meet you at the tetrahedral's shed, right away."

"Right!" said Poodle, and walked away, with a military salute. He smiled a broad, cheerful, slightly insulting smile at the band of waiters and water-boys, who were still watching him suspiciously.

As soon as he had got hold of Lieutenant Adeler, by telephone, he hurried to the tetrahedral's shed, and started filling her fuel tank, looking after her oil, and polishing the search-light lens.

The General arrived at eight, with two soldiers—an old sergeant, who had fought hand-to-hand with Indians and Filipinos, in a dozen battles; and a husky young private, who had a record as a prize-fighter.

From the Hotel de Suisse, they received a message that Captain Welch and Jolls had started out in a motor car, at about six.

"Let her go," said the General, at that.

Lieutenant Jack Adeler got ready to take the pilot's seat in the *Hustle*, but General Thorne said, "I think my young friend Darby, here, would like to run your aeroplane. Wouldn't you, Torrington? Ah, I thought so. Go ahead, then."

To the Lieutenant he explained, "Mr. Adeler, it's like this. If you smashed us up—of course we *will* get smashed up, flying in this harum-scarum way, at night, it would be rank insubordination. Lieutenants really ought not to kill Generals. Or, if you want me to be serious with you, I think that young Darby here, by his work to-day, has put himself right on a level with young Griffin, and you, and I am quite serious in saying that I couldn't give him higher praise."

Poodle blushed, as he took the levers. The *Hustle* bumped down the roadway, lighted by the search-light, and joltingly launched out into the darkness.

He was rather trembly, but he was glad, too. What could be a greater lark than to rescue Hike, good old Hike!

He sang to himself as he left the Potomac and, with the search-light on, swung over to the road which he had followed earlier in the day.

When he had reached a spot about half a mile from the hill where Hike was imprisoned, Poodle suddenly switched off all lights, shot the *Hustle* up to three thousand feet, snapped off the motor, and made a long glide toward the top of the hill. For the first time, he wished that cool Hike were at the levers, instead of him. It was a terrific strain. Silent as a night-flying owl, yet with a swift drop, the *Hustle* shot down toward the top of the hill. The many planes creaked quietly. Then they circled, and landed in the fields just beyond the marshes at the bottom of the hill, all so quietly that none of the guards could have heard them.

They climbed out, and filed through the marshes. The General, who had so cheerfully acted as merely a passenger while on the *Hustle*, took charge, and with quick, sharp, whispered orders led them through the mud and brush to the foot of the hill.

"Adeler, you and the soldiers stay here. Darby and I will climb up and try to get on the roof of the cabin. Thatched—we can hear through it. When I light a match up there, you charge up and get into the fight. We'll capture Captain Welch, if I find that he's guilty of plotting with Jolls. We'll have to let the others go—we have no civil warrant for them. But we can damage them a little, and set the police on them directly. Come on, Darby—you'll have to lead up, you know the lay of the land."

The General had been used to an easy life, these last few years, but it kept Poodle hurrying, crawling on his stomach up through the grass and shrubs, to keep ahead of him. Once, when their heads were near each other, he could make out that the General's jaws were set like iron.

They stole up to the cabin, and heard the five guards lazily talking near the door, in front.

"Give me a leg up," hissed the General, and climbed the low back wall, clutching at the thatch of the roof, and dragging himself up. He thrust down a hand to Poodle and pulled him after; then the two of them lay flat as shingles on the roof, for a guard was just meandering about the cabin, humming.

The General was still panting from his exertions; and he whispered to Poodle, "Well, young man, what do you think of a man of my age and rank crawling up cabins that don't even belong to me, as though I were a boy shinning up a tree for apples!" But he didn't seem very angry, as he patted Poodle on the shoulder.

With slightly raised head, Poodle leaned on his elbows, digging down into the rotten old thatch. He had to lift out all the straw, lest it fall through and give them away to any one beneath. But in a few moments he had a sizable hole, through which they could listen to anything that went on within the cabin.

It was time they *were* listening!

Four of the five guards had entered the cabin. A stocky man addressed by the others as Bat was arguing with a sleezy fellow called Snafflin. "Aw thunder," Bat was urging, "give the kid a little while longer, Snafflin, you whopperjawed jackass."

"Look here, you mutton-head" (Snafflin really called him something much worse, but what he said would better not be repeated here), "you know what the Boss said; 'Give him till eight o'clock. Then if he won't come around and write the letter, tie him up in the swamp.' It's way after eight now, and either you tie him up or— Well, there'll be a new leader in this cute little band of cutthroats, savvy?"

"Speak for yourself—about being a cutthroat, Snafflin. Me, there is one throat I hope to cut—yours. One of these days I'll *get* you, Snafflin, just remember that. Now—well, you guys are four to one. We'll tie up the kid."

Then, speaking to Hike, Bat continued:

"Kid, I'm sure sorry I've got to do this. Cummon now, won't you sign the letter? Aw, cummon!"

"Nope, Bat, I can't do it. Sorry." Poodle could just make out Hike's tired smile as he said it, tied up, down there in the frowsy cabin.

"So'm I sorry. Well, kid, here goes."

The door opened, and Poodle and the General could see the four men leading out Hike, while the fifth man, still on guard, brought up the rear, rifle on his arm. Hike, with his feet hobbled and his wrists tied tight, stumbled along weakly.

Poodle whispered to the General, "I'll sneak down and let him loose, and beat it back up here."

"Good. Go ahead."

Poodle was already sliding down the thatch, and crawling after the thugs and their victim. In the thick bank of weeds at the edge of the woods, he nestled comfortably, and grinned as he thought how horribly fooled were the five thugs there, who were tying up Hike so securely. They were talking quietly, taking it for granted that no one nearer than Washington had any idea what they were up to. In the light of the lanterns they carried, Poodle could see them pass a heavy line about Hike many times, fastening him to a fir of prickly, uncomfortable bark, which would scratch Hike every time he moved. Hike's feet were left in thick mud; and away from him stretched pools thick with mosquitoes. Even Poodle, with his hands free to brush them away, was terribly annoyed by these pests, as he crouched and waited; and when he thought of Hike, trying to drive them off, with his hands tight bound, and his skin scratched by the bark every time he moved, gentle Poodle wanted very much to kill the whole bunch.

The thugs filed away, talking (Poodle could hear them) of whether "The Boss"—probably P. J. Jolls—would leave Hike there to die, or release him. "He'll never sign that letter, that's sure," said Bat. "Well, he might 'a' done it if it hadn't been for your blankety blank butting in," snarled Snafflin. Poodle saw Bat stop, calmly raise a lantern, and look at Snafflin, till those vicious, yellowed eyes were turned away.

Then Poodle slipped into the muddy edge of the marsh; hastily crawled through to Hike, and whistled low, adding "Shhhh!" He pulled out his little penknife, and hacked away at the bonds, with Hike busily pulling at the cord as it frayed through. So at last Hike stood free, beside the thorny-barked fir. For a moment he staggered. Then he abruptly sat down, in the wet brush. Poodle sat down beside him. They shook hands; not saying a word as yet, and with one accord these aviators, these meddlers with Army Boards and wealthy manufacturers, burst softly into the highly grown-up and dignified Santa Benicia Freshman Class song; written by that excellent young poet Mr. Poodle Darby:

> "We stung 'em, see? We stung 'em, see?
> Oh, the Soph-o-mores are wild.
> She tied the train to a jim-jam tree,
> But we wept and chid the child.
> We wept and chewed the chilled ice cream,
> And oh, but she had a pain.
> So we climbed in a team and we dreamed us a dream
> She had untied the train."

"H. G. Griffin," remarked Poodle, "if you can't find anything better to do at this crisis than to sing things like that, I think you'd better just jolly well get tied up again. There's Jack Adeler and two sojers over across the clearing waiting for the General's signal, and General Thorne is lying on top of the cabin, getting his trousers all nice and dirty with thatch, and saying 'O cuss! O trunions!' every time he slaps a mosquito. And here you beat it into this very nasty swamp to study nature."

"Poodle, my son, you are a jackass," were Hike's first words to his rescuer.

"Hike, my child, you are a goat," was Poodle's retort; after which they solemnly shook hands again, stopped being boys for a while, and Poodle hastily led the way to the Lieutenant and his soldiers, where Hike was to wait and join the charge on the cabin.

Poodle hastened back to his nook on the thatch. He was hardly in place, beside the hole through the roof, when excitement began in the dingy room beneath.

CHAPTER XV

CHARGE!

"THOSE guards out of the way, all right? What's that behind that pile of furniture?" Captain Welch was talking to P. J. Jolls, in the lonely cabin on the hill, while Poodle and General Thorne listened through a hole in the thatch.

"You're pretty nervous for an Army officer, strikes me. That's a shadow behind that furniture, and that's all. Of course if you want me to take it away, it would give me pleas—" Mr. P. J. Jolls voice was filled with contempt.

"Well, you'll get nervous if you don't watch out. 'Fact, I think you will right now, Jolls, for it's about time to tell you what I want before we go any farther. I want you to boost my seventy-five thousand to a hundred and fifty thousand dollars."

"Whew!" commented the General, on the roof. "That might be almost called a bribe! So that's why Welch wanted us to take Jolls' aeroplanes!"

"Whew!" Jolls was ejaculating below, like an echo. "Say, what do you think I'm made of? Why, even seventy-five thousand is too much. I won't make a cent over a hundred thousand clear profit on the contract, even as it is, even if the Board grants a full million; and if you get seventy-five thousand, I'll get only twenty-five. And a hundred and fifty thousand, why, that will just mean fifty thousand coming out of my pocket."

"Oh, cut that. You're lying, and I know it, and you know I know it. I may be nervous but I'm not afraid of you or your hired thugs—private detectives, you like to call 'em; murderers I call 'em. I'm sorry I ever went into this fool business; even if I do need the money for that gambling debt, and even if I do hate those goody-goody fools like Jack Adeler and that old woman General Thorne—with his knitting."

(Just then this same General Thorne, not so very many feet away from Captain Welch, was clinching and unclinching his plump hands as though he had hold of some one's throat. Poodle was busily stuffing his handkerchief into his mouth.)

Captain Welch was going on, "I'm not in this for my health. You know that if we get found out I'll be the most disgraced man in America—next to you. But I'm getting desperate anyway. Desperate, do you hear me? That gambling affair, and the shortage in accounts at Fort Myer (I'd like to kill you for finding that out)—they'll come out if I can't get hold of plenty of hush-money. And then I'll have to have enough over so I can resign from the Army and go to Europe for the rest of my life. I'm desperate I tell you. Now either you come across, or I'll split to General Thorne—tell him the whole business by letter, and make a getaway from the country. It's easy enough for me to move—I haven't got any factories like you to take with me, and I'll be welcomed in at least three South American armies. Here's my ultimatum: Sign up for a hundred and fifty-thousand, or I walk out of this cabin—with my revolver out and the drop on you and your thugs—"

"ALL RIGHT!" snarled Jolls. "Take your bribe." And he signed a small sheet of paper which the Captain tucked into his pocket.

Poodle was surprised to hear something much like a repressed chuckle beside him; and the General whispered, "It's lovely—it's *lovely*! I've already heard enough to land Captain Welch in disgrace."

"Well, now," Jolls was saying, below, "let's get our lines straight, and then we can talk to this Griffin boy. Young whelp! I'd like to kill him just on general principles. First, we'll make him sign that letter. I think an hour in the swamp will have him about where we want him. Then to-night I'll have Bat do the second-story burglar act, and steal all the plans of the tetra-hedral that there are here in Washington—at the Lieutenant's room and the patent office. That last is the most dangerous thing yet. As for Priest, you've got the data on his having been arrested for forgery have you?"

"Yes," said Welch.

"Is that true—was Martin Priest a forger?" the General hastily whispered to Poodle.

"Yes, he confessed it to Lieutenant Adeler and us," admitted Poodle.

The General answered, "Then it's all right, and we'll just forget it."

Below, Jolls was going on with his plot:

"We'll let that get into the newspapers, and at the same time we'll send Priest young Griffin's letter, and a faked letter from the General, and enough other stuff like that to make him think he's disgraced and he'll just disappear. I've had my men studying him closely enough so that I know he's pretty sensitive. I don't think we'll have any more trouble with him. You still feel that the electric firearms he carries make him too dangerous to attack directly?"

"Yes," again said Captain Welch.

"Well, all right, but I wish we could kill him."

"Yes, it *is* too bad his appetite for raw meat's spoiled," Poodle whispered, like a "little cherub that sits up aloft."

Jolls was going on: "And you'll 'tend to burning up the tetrahedral all right, will you? Well, that's fixed. I guess that will cover it so that we won't hear anything more. The only things we've got to look out for are Adeler and that Torrington boy—no, Torrington Darby I guess his name is. Well, he's not dangerous—he's one of these fat little innocents. We'll let him alone."

"*Thanks*," that "fat little innocent" softly crooned, on the roof.

"I guess young Griffin will keep his mouth shut before we get through with him. 'Fact, I wouldn't mind having him tied up in the swamp till he went clean crazy and never could talk again," said Jolls, coldly.

"Neither would I—young imp," snapped the Captain.

"What I'll do to you, sweet Captain," the General murmured, on the roof.

"That leaves Adeler. I'll have to devise some way to fix him—we might just suggest to Bat that he'd better disappear—but I wouldn't like to kill any one," Mr. Jolls spoke very sentimentally.

"Oh, no," said Captain Welch, sarcastically, "I know how tender-hearted you are. But do what you please—so long as I get the hundred and fifty thou. and can get out of the country."

"Arrangements look all right to you?" Jolls asked.

"Yes," said Welch.

"Well, then, let's go down and have a look at young Griffin. You remember to see that not a shred of the tetrahedral is left. (Say, call the guards, will you, now?) Run a fuse into its fuel tank or just sprinkle kerosene over —"

While Jolls was thus giving final directions, his thugs were summoned; and then, very suddenly, there was "something doing."

The General stood straight up, and lighted, not one signal-match, but a whole box, flinging them flaming up into the air. A moment before he had seemed a rather puffy, quiet old man, but now he was changed into a red-hot fighting devil. He tore away at the thatch, with his revolver-butt.

Poodle caught up great handfuls of the old straw, too, and as the General dropped through on the astounded seven men below, Poodle dropped with him, revolver in hand.

As he landed on the floor of the cabin, the General toppled over and sank to his knees. He had turned an ankle. But, kneeling, he covered the Captain, just as the Captain drew a revolver of his own. For a second no one moved; Poodle, Jolls, the guards at the door, all stood with held breath, while the General on his knees and the Captain standing covered each other with their guns. Then Jolls picked up a chair and swung it high over the General's head, behind.

Poodle forgot his own revolver and swiftly adopted class-rush tactics. Swinging his leg about, he kicked Mr. Jolls in the puffy fat ankles, just once. That was enough. The business man dropped the chair with an "Ouch" as foolish as the squeak of a mouse.

Just then there was a commotion at the door. The guards faced about, and right into them charged Jack Adeler and his armed aids. The guards rushed out.

Through the window slid Hike Griffin, tottering from his exposure, but a very grim look on his face. He dropped fairly on top of the astonished Captain, caught the revolver with his toe, and sent it hurtling to the roof. The General was up instantly, and roared to Captain Welch and Jolls, "Into that corner there, or I'll fire." The two plotters backed into a corner, and the General kept them both covered.

Three of the guards were covered by the Lieutenant and his soldiers. One was down and out from a soldier's club-blow. But Snafflin had dropped on his stomach and was wriggling off through the grass. From an outside corner of the cabin, scarcely seen in the dim light from scattered lanterns, he carefully aimed his revolver at the Lieutenant.

Just then Bat—one of those covered by the Lieutenant's men—made a flying leap toward the corner of the house. One of the soldiers fired, and the bullet took Bat in the shoulder. But Bat caught Snafflin's wrist, and rolled over in the grass, still feebly holding the revolver. As he let it go, Hike darted over and fell upon Snafflin, catching him full in the face with his fist. He got a wrestler's half-Nelson on Snafflin, and before the thug could recover, Poodle had slipped a pair of handcuffs on him.

The General now marched out his two chief plotters, and made a short, sweet speech to all of them:

"You gentlemen—I'll have to let you all go—including your chief rascal, Mr. Jolls. I have no civil warrant for your arrest—didn't have time to get one. I apologize for the neglect. But I'll have warrants issued at once. Jolls, I'll not only have you arrested, but I'll see that every bit of the news about your plans is given to the Associated Press, and that you are disgraced for life. You, Captain Welch, I place you under arrest. You will come with us. You needn't be told what will happen to you. There's one of your thugs who has saved the Lieutenant's life—I saw the incident through the door."

The General pointed to Bat, and Hike said, "Bat's his name. He was kind to me when I was tied up—mighty kind. Wanted to let me go. I'd like to see him freed."

The General continued, "Well, the rest of you—except Captain Welch and Bat—you can all lay down your revolvers and get out of that gate. You'd better make the best time you can, for permit me to warn you that I'll have the best detectives in the country on your trail as soon as warrants are issued."

Four of the five hired thugs, with Jolls at their head, hastily sneaked down the hill, toward the place where Jolls' automobile had been left. (They were destined to have a cheerful little disappointment for the Lieutenant had found the automobile, while waiting for the signal, and, being in uniform, had been able to send the chauffeur flying off to town, by threatening to arrest him.)

The victors were left with Bat and the Captain. The latter stood sulkily waiting. Bat was sitting on the grass, with Poodle tying up the injured shoulder with a strip of his own shirt sleeve. Up to him came Hike, exclaiming, "Bat, old man, I'd like to shake hands with you."

"*All* right, kid," said Bat, cheerfully, "I'd jus' soon—but take my left wing. T'other just got on the bum. I was picking a bullet out of the air—like baseball."

"Bat," said the General, "I'd like to have you make—what do you call it? Oh—I'd like to have you 'make a getaway.' Have you any money?"

"About ten dollars."

"Well, here's forty. That will help some. Now promise me you'll get away as quickly as you can. I'll see that the detectives don't search for you as hard as they do for the others, but your connection with the gang will get you into trouble unless you get good and far away from here."

"I'll do it, sir," declared Bat. "Thanks for the forty. I'll beat it."

He rose, rather dizzily, shook hands with Hike silently, and headed for the gate. Then the captors turned to their prisoner, Captain Welch.

He faced them, grimly. He had not given up the game yet.

CHAPTER XVI

THE CAPTAIN'S TRICK

THERE were three very quiet persons as the victors hastened back to Washington in the *Hustle*, driven by Lieutenant Adeler. The General was nursing his twisted ankle; Hike was lying still, with Poodle occasionally patting him on the shoulder. And Captain Welch, between the two soldiers, sat with his head on his knees. There were no handcuffs on him, but his revolver had been taken away.

As the tetrahedral fluttered down to its aerodrome, in Washington, the Captain stood up wearily. He seemed too tired to move. The two soldiers guarding him thought they would have an easy time. They plodded along beside him, silent.

Suddenly Hike, dragging himself along beside the others, made a leap and caught at the Captain's arm.

It was too late. The Captain had already swallowed the liquid of a small bottle which he had drawn from his inner vest-pocket. He threw up his arms, cried out once, and sank in a pathetic heap.

Hike picked up the bottle, turned to the astonished General, and said, "Poison. Prussic acid. Works instantly, doesn't it?"

Bending over the Captain, the General felt his heart. "Not dead yet," he cried. "We may save him. You—" pointing to a soldier, "get an auto *quick!*"

The soldier stopped the car of a passer-by, who consented to take them to the General's house. They roared by a policeman—with warning, uplifted hand—as though he didn't exist. Down the streets, under the arc lights, they thundered, and drew up at the General's house.

Poodle and the two soldiers had been left behind—to come on afterward. Hike and the General and the Lieutenant lifted out Captain Welch, and carried him into the house. He was left on a couch.

The General bustled into another room, to telephone for a doctor. Hike sat beside the couch, feeling the Captain's pulse, while the Lieutenant was searching through the General's cabinet, upstairs, for a medicine that would bring the Captain to. The room was very quiet. Hike felt himself nodding away, unable to keep awake, even now, when in the presence of what looked like death.

Through half-closed eyelids, he suddenly saw the Captain sit up, fling his legs off the couch, and aim a blow with closed fist.

Hike ducked and hit back, but the Captain rushed to a window—open to the summer night—and leaped out.

Dashing to the window, Hike saw him run around the corner. He yelled to the Lieutenant and the General, and started for the door.

"Captain's escaped. Went through window," he bawled from the doorstep, and hurried down the stairs. There was not a sign of the Captain in the streets about.

The General, Hike and Adeler ran in different directions—but no trace of Welch. He had probably caught a trolley-car, or a taxicab, on a busy street near by. They finally gave up the chase and gathered at the General's house.

"My ankle is *very* sore after this last run," said the General angrily. "The next time I try to handle prisoners myself—well, I won't."

"It was my fault," Hike began.

"Of *course*!" said the General. "I ought to expect you, after you've been through an experience that would kill most youngsters, to capture the Captain, single-handed! Mr. Adeler, what's your idea of how Welch got over prussic acid so quickly as that?"

"It's a mystery to me," said Jack Adeler, wearily.

"I've got an idea," said Hike. "I don't believe that *was* prussic acid! Here's the bottle. Couldn't it be tested?"

He fished the vial out of his side pocket. He had picked it up when the Captain dropped it.

"Good boy!" roared the General. "Of course! But let's try it. I don't think I've forgotten all my chemistry, and I've a small laboratory here. Any liquid left in the bottle?"

"A couple of drops."

"Let's see it." The General, limping, led the way to a small laboratory he had upstairs. Silently the other two watched him test the few drops left. At last he tossed the vial into a basket, laughing.

"That's about as much prussic acid as I am. It's pure water! Well. *Well!*"

The General seated himself wearily in a straight-backed wooden chair, then started up and exclaimed, "Can't I even have a comfortable chair, after all this? Come on down to the library. Mr. Adeler, we'll have a couple of cigars. Do you smoke, you, young Griffin? No? Well, I'm glad to hear you don't."

When they were all seated in the great library, the General mused:

"Well, we've been busy to-night. It isn't much after midnight, but it's all over. By the way, Mr. Adeler, did you telephone those orders to the police-station to have the tetrahedral's house, and your rooms, watched? That's good. Some of those thugs might make trouble yet.

"But I don't think they will. I think we'll have them all in jail in a few hours. Jolls included. As for Captain Welch—it doesn't make much difference whether we catch him or not. He'll be disgraced and kicked out of the Army just the same. In fact, I think we might as well drop the 'Captain' from his name, and call him plain 'Welch,' from now on. He's a private citizen—and without honor.

"As for the tetrahedral, I think that the Board will have adopted that as the Army model by noon to-morrow. You can telegraph Mr. Priest, at once.

"Well, that's about all." The General's official sternness disappeared, and he became a gentle, humorous old man. "And now, where is that young Darby? I think that at least I might have him here, to talk to. He's the only one I've ever met with sufficient sense of humor to understand my grievances.

"Here I've comported myself with a fair amount of dignity as a high-ranking army officer for some years. And what happens to-night? I ride in night-flying infernal contrivances. I fight mosquitoes on a ridiculous thatch-roof. I get covered with dirt—and I associate with other persons like you two, who are about equally dirty. I sprain my ankle dropping through a hole, as though I were an actor in a moving-picture company. I kill captains and don't kill them dead. I act like a second lieutenant who got out of the Point about three years too early.

"But there is one thing that I trust I may be able to do with more dignity and efficiency. That is sleeping! Now, you gentlemen are not going to stir one step out of the house to-night. You are to sleep right here. Mr. Adeler, will you please ring for a servant?"

And so Hike got to bed, and slept till noon next day. It was, perhaps, the most satisfactory thing he had ever done in his life, to pull off the clothes fouled with the mud of the swamp, drop into a tub of hot water, and then crawl between clean sheets. He may have made some fair speed, in his day, with the tetrahedral; but that was as nothing compared with the magnificent speed with which he slept. He declared to Poodle, next day, that he had broken all records, by sleeping at a rate of not less than one hundred knots an hour.

One other had been awake, however, and when Hike awoke, about the noon of the following day, there was handed to him a note, mailed late the night before, which had been addressed to him in care of General Thorne.

The note ran:

"DEAR GERALD GRIFFIN:

"You may be pleased to learn that I shall not forget the debt I owe to you and to Lieutenant Adeler. Believe me, my dear Gerald, I shall have the pleasure of getting even with both of you, in the best manner which shall present itself. I am writing in order to give you the joy of watching for trouble every day and hour.

"Believe me, your very obedient servant,

"WILLOUGHBY WELCH, U. S. A."

Hike read the note twice, then yawned, "So Wibbelty-Wobbelty wants to scare us, eh? How unkind!" He turned over and slept peacefully for another hour.

He was awakened by a call from Poodle, who shouted, "Say, Bat has gone and confessed to the government about how they were going to try to rob the Patent Office, and the federal secret service is after Jolls and his thugs, already. And say, the Army Board has telegraphed Priest, accepting the tetrahedral."

"Good. Have they got Captain Welch?"

"No. I guess he made his getaway."

"Too bad. Because I'm awful' scared. Here's a note from him."

Poodle read through the note, and asked anxiously.

"Aw, he's just kidding, isn't he, Hike?"

"No. I don't think he is."

"Gee. Aren't you worried?"

"Not much," smiled Hike, and he looked it. "What worries me a whole lot more," he continued, "is that we'll have to get back to Santa Benicia Academy, in a few days—and oh! how the fellows will kid us, for getting conspicuous, and us only Sophomores. That's the real thing to worry about."

"Um-*huh*," agreed Poodle, gloomily.

CHAPTER XVII

AT SANTA BENICIA ACADEMY

SANTA BENICIA MILITARY ACADEMY, California. It is a peaceful, beautiful place, with no signs of hurrying tetrahedrals or busy Army Boards. White and purple figs overhang the walk to the main building, and beside it there are little stretches of grass, shaded by orange trees, or tulip trees filled with great white blossoms. Keep along the walk, and you come to the Yard, surrounded by vine-covered dormitories. Beyond the Yard are the stretches of the athletic field and parade ground. Everywhere are palms, and grape vines, and giant roses. A beautiful place, and an ideal school for boys. For, even though it is a military academy, there are practically no rules. The students are expected to be gentlemen—there are no "bounds," almost no "hours."

Messrs. Hike Griffin and Poodle Darby trotted through the Yard gate, their arms about each other's shoulders, singing the newly revised class song:

> "We stung 'em, see? we stung 'em, see?
> Oh, the Jun-i-ors are wild."

They were trying to look peacefully happy. But they were not happy in the least. Poodle put it right when he said they felt like clams who had strayed out of their rivers and gotten fried, and then tried to go back to the mud and pretend they'd never seen a stove.

For every chap who passed them, except for the new Freshmen, shouted something like this: "Hello, aviators. Brought your airyplane? When do I get a ride?"

Poodle admitted that they felt "like digging a hole and crawling into it, and pulling the hole in after them," when the great Pink Eye Morrison, president of the Senior Class, and baseball-captain, stopped, raised his school cap to them, and remarked:

"It isest a great honor you doest us poor slobs, O thou Griffin and thou Darby in the vocative, to visit us in the midst of—"

"Oh, *please* cheese it," begged Hike, and Pink Eye passed on, with an unholy smile.

That is but a sample of what they got, not only from the Juniors and Seniors, but even from their own classmates. It had been a joy, in the morning, to drop their suit-cases on the grass, and yell at their old friends of the year before, but by afternoon, they felt like keeping to their rooms. It looked as if they were going to have a horrible year, as if everything they said or did would be laughed at, as coming from "the aviators." They wished, for a while, that they had never seen an aeroplane.

Poodle tried to convince Hike and himself that it was all nonsense for two persons who had just been playing with tetrahedral-flights and generals and million-dollar Army appropriations, to be bothered by a few laughs from classmates. But they were bothered, just the same.

There is something about school honors that make them mean more than anything else. A fellow has been working for them ever since the day he got out of the kindergarten and put on knickers. Perhaps that's the reason. Anyway, Hike and Poodle, after having played the game hard all Freshman year, and having made good, were broken-hearted at starting in the Sophomore year queered.

"Queered" they seemed to be. Every one was ready to "jolly" them. Partly, it was envy and jealousy on the part of the fellows; partly it was a feeling that these two Sophomores had broken every unwritten law of the school by making themselves so conspicuous in the newspapers. But mostly it was the joy of being able to torment such famous people. Never was a West Point plebe so badly hazed as was the late General Frederick Dent Grant, when he entered the Point as the son of General Ulysses Grant, President of the United States. Hike and Poodle remembered that they, too, had taken delight in "kidding" a classmate of theirs who was the son of the Governor of Nevada—just because he was the son of a governor.

Probably Plebe Grant and the son of the Governor would gladly have traded their positions as the sons of great men for good reputations with their classes. So it was with Hike and Poodle. The problem before them, they decided, as they entered their room, was twice as hard as fighting any old P. J. Jolls. They had to win over the school.

The room was filled with memories of Freshman year—Hike had come back to it after helping win the Freshman game with San Dinero; Poodle had here written his poems for the school magazine; here they had "ground" for the spring examinations. Hike's football-helmet hung over the fireplace—where, in the chilly California evenings, they had had many a good fire, with classmates singing and talking.

Sitting on the broad window-seat, they could look across the silver stretch of the Carquinez Straits to purple Mount Diablo. Here they had lounged so many lazy afternoons, with friends, planning walking-trips across to the mountain. But now—?

They were pretty silent, for a gloomy half-hour, while unpacking; wandering around the room, hanging up a photograph of the *Hustle* here, and tossing a new soft-cushion there, and fighting over nails for toothbrushes and bars for towels. Poodle came near sniffling, as he spread a new couch-cover out carefully, patting out the wrinkles, and remembering that when his pretty sister had given it to him, a couple of days before, she had said, "I hope you and all your friends will be willing to rest on this, Torry, when you get tired of being heroes."

"O rats, what's the use," said Hike suddenly. "But maybe they'll quit kidding us, in a couple of days. What's that!"

"That" was a curious sound beneath their windows, down in the Yard. Shouts of "Tie your struts to the dingbat," and "Curl your legs around the levers and get a purchase on them" mingled with the crack of a motor. Rushing to the window, they saw a group of classmates about the strangest aeroplane that ever was built. Before a stationary motorcycle was Left Eared Dongan, Sophomore, the wild-haired candidate for football-end, seated in a Morris chair carted out from some one's room. He wore a child's toy helmet and a huge wooden sword, and was busily twiddling levers the size of a large man's body. Beside him was a classmate stuffed with pillows, and bearing on his back a placard lettered "Poodle." Behind them, for the wings of this remarkable aeroplane, a blanket was stretched between two wooden chairs.

Out from an entryway rushed three boys wearing masks and brandishing clubs. Left Eared Dongan shut off the motorcycle's motor, stood up, waved his wooden sword wildly and yelled in a pleasant, refined voice which could have been heard across the Carquinez Straits, "On! brave Poodle, have at them. The King of Salamanca awaits our coming."

The mock Poodle got up with great dignity, and snapped a toy pistol at the brigands, three times. They fell flat, with considerable kicking of the legs, and bawled for mercy.

The few windows that had not been occupied by the heads of grinning Santa Benicians were well filled now. From all 'round the quadrangle came shouts of "Flee, brave Hike," "Try your auxiliary motor," "On to China," "Touch-down with your southeast plane."

Then came from the entry a fat boy with a false mustache, bearing the sign "President Taft." He fell on his knees before Left Eared Dongan and sang out, "Take me with you, O Hike. I nominate thee a second-hand major general."

The group danced cheerfully about the aeroplane, while Left Eared Dongan settled back in his Morris chair and started the motor again.

Hike and Poodle smiled feebly, up there. But they did not smile, they most certainly did not, when they were left out of the Fig Tree Celebration, that evening.

On the office-walk was a huge tree called "Fig Tree Major." Under this was held annually the solemn ceremony which officially began the hazing of the Freshmen. Each of the new students was put through his paces by a Master of Ceremonies and a Jester, while the class applauded.

The Class President of the year before was usually chosen Master of Ceremonies, and this year Hike and Poodle had practically taken it for granted that they would be chosen Master and Jester.

They were not. The class, marching across the Yard, did not call them out of their rooms. "Bluggy" Blodgett, center rush of the Freshman team of the year before, had been chosen Master; and Left Eared Dongan was Jester.

It took some nerve for Hike and Poodle to go to the Fig Tree Celebration, after that cut, but they went—and nearly every classmate that spoke to them said something insulting about aviating.

They were very unhappy as they sat in their room, after the Celebration and the first hazing of the Freshmen.

"Gee," growled Hike, "I wonder if they're going to keep it up all year!"

There was a modest tapping at the door.

"Come in!"

Mousey Tincom, a small wisp of a Sophomore, who played chess and studied hard and worshiped Hike as he did Napoleon (whom Mousey thought he himself resembled, and whom he sure didn't resemble), came ambling in, sat carefully on the front edge of a large chair, and bleated:

"Hello, fellows. I'm awful' sorry about to-night."

"The class going to keep it up?" asked Poodle.

"I'm afraid so. Left Ear was 'lowing we haven't had so good an opening for jollying any one since the Flood. Say, I've got some news for you."

"All right. We can stand it." (Hike was impolite. You had to be impolite to Mousey Tincom, or he would have stood about worshiping all the while.)

"Well, you know Captain Thurbey got off'n the job as military instructor last spring, and they hadn't appointed any one till just now. Now, I hear that Lieutenant Adeler of the Signal Corps—"

"HurRAY!" shouted Poodle and Hike. "Go on."

"Well, he's asked the President to transfer him here, so he can make some experiments with wireless and televises in the laboratory here. So I think he'll be military instructor here. Is he nice?"

"Slickest chap that ever woggled a saber, Jack Adeler is," said Poodle, and Hike agreed "You bet."

"Well, say, some one was telling me—listen across there! they must be hazing the Freshmen good and plenty to-night; making them aviate, sounds like."

"Hang the aviating—though I suppose that's what we'll get right along," sighed Poodle. "Gwan about Lieutenant Adeler."

"Well, some one was saying that he's here already—came this afternoon, and that he's staying at the Headmaster's to-night."

"I wonder why he hasn't let us know?" wondered Hike.

"Probably wants to surprise us," mused Poodle.

"Well," said Hike, "I've got some unpacking to do, Mousey."

"All right, so long you fellows. I'll have to beat it and help the hazing, I guess." And Mousey disappeared.

For the thousandth time Poodle declared that Hike was intolerably rude to poor Mousey, and for the thousandth time Hike declared, "Yuh, I know I'm beastly to him, but if you'd ever come in from a dusty practise game and seen Mousey hanging around and admiring, standing there like he was waiting for a hand-out—just when you felt grouchy anyway, why you'd want to kill him. He'd be here all the time if—"

Light, quick feet on the stairs, a tap at the door, and in came—Lieutenant Jack Adeler!

Hike and Poodle arose and beat him on the back till he could scarcely breathe, half laughing and half crying with joy.

"Yes," he answered their questions, which were piled on him like a brick-wall falling, "I'll be here all year. Want to make some experiments. The military part here won't take much time. And I'll have the pleasure of getting even with you two young fiends for mixing me up with Welch and Jolls. Oh, the way I'll hector you on the parade-ground—! By the way, speaking of Jolls, his trial ought to come off pretty soon."

Then Messrs. Griffin and Darby suddenly changed from Santa Benicians to *very* grown-up aviators, and plunged into a long talk with Jack Adeler.

But when the Lieutenant had gone, when Taps had sounded and they were undressing, in the dark, they changed back into two very tired youngsters, horribly bored at the thought of being "jollied" all that year.

They seemed to have guessed right. Though Hike was immediately tried out at half on the school team, for two weeks they had to keep to themselves as much as possible. The school wits found a hundred new ways of referring to aviation, every day.

CHAPTER XVIII

THE GREAT HAZING

Tune: Son of a Gambolier.
Oh, I'm an aviator, I'm a number seven slob,
And when it comes to heroism, I am on the job.
The only way that ordinary mutts can mix with me
Is take me out and haze me till I lose my dignity.
CHORUS:
I'm a son of a son of a son of a son of a son of an aeronaut,
And I have sworn to lie no more about the fights I've fought,
And I'm so jolly thankful to the Seniors who have taught,
I'm the son of a son of a son of a son of a son of an airy-naught!

Oh, I'm so jolly thankful that these ordinary mutts
Have spanked me good and plenty with my tetrahedral struts,
And I have promised not to let my head get big again,
When I go aviating on my airy aeroplane.

SUCH was the song that sounded below the windows of Hike and Poodle, as they sat studying in their room, at ten of the evening.

"This is getting to be too much," growled Hike. "Some one's going to get hurt."

Poodle looked at him shyly. He scarcely knew this savage, stern young man, this new Hike.

There was a sound as of many boys talking all at once, below; then Pink Eye Morrison, president of the Senior Class, rushed in.

"The Seniors below," he panted. "You fellows are to come down and get hazed—good and plenty!"

"Say, this is a little too much," said Hike, quietly. "I'm getting pretty fairly tired of this being kidded for having done fairly decent work with a machine that most of you fellows would be scared to look at. Come ahead, you fellows, and I'll lick as many of you as I can. But hazed—*us, Sophomores*? No, indeed. Ring off—you've got the wrong number."

"Why, you poor nut—" began Pink Eye, when Poodle interrupted.

"Say, Hike, you've got the wrong idea. This is a Hazing Extraordinary, isn't it, Morrison?"

Pink Eye nodded. Poodle went on:

"Don't you remember hearing about how a Sophomore got hazed by the Senior Class two years ago, because he was really a darn nice fellow, only everybody was kidding him, and the Seniors wanted the kidding to wind up in a grand jamboree, and then stop? Stop absolute. Ain't that the idea here, Morrison?"

"Of *course*," snapped Pink Eye. "No more references to aviation after tonight unless you want them. Why, Hike, you young goat, do you suppose we'd honor you with a Hazing Extraordinary and take the trouble to stop all this kidding unless we liked you?"

Hike held out his hand to Pink Eye, and gave him one of his rarest smiles —one of those smiles so filled with strength and kindness and affection that no one could resist.

"I was a fool," said he.

"'S all right," said Morrison. "Hustle up, you fellows, get into pink pajamas—or blue or something, if you haven't got pink—and come on. The theory of a Hazing Extraordinary is that we crooly snatch you out of bed, see?"

Below, the Seniors were singing the hazing-ditty again, and bellowing, "On with 'em. Where's the victims. Hurry 'em, Pink Eye."

The Seniors were led by the most prominent boys in the class—fellows like Pink Eye, president of the class; the noble Taffy Bingham, champion wrestler of the school and right tackle of the school team; Gimlet Jones, the prize scholar, who would probably win the school scholarship, that year, and go to Yale; Bunk Tarver, football player and class clown; and big Bill McDever, captain of the school football-team.

Finally, Hike and Poodle appeared below, followed by a crowd of underclassmen, wondering what was up; marveling at the hazing of Sophomores.

The culprits were marched out to the open space behind Fig Tree Major, where the Senior Class formed in a ring. Behind them appeared the Juniors, with Sophomores at the rear, keeping the Freshmen back.

Pink Eye Morrison had put on a foolish wig and a more foolish black gown, hastily made out of a deceased overcoat-lining. He sat on his haunches, the most dignified judge that ever scowled at a criminal. Taffy Bingham, the wrestler, was the State's Attorney; Gimlet Jones, Santa Benicia's prize scholar, the attorney for the prisoners.

"May it please Your Dishonor," orated Taffy Bingham, "the State charges these two wang-footed chumps with criminal conspiracy against the peace and class-feeling of Santa Benicia Academy. By indulging in actions which have given them wide notoriety, they have shown their opinion that a Sophomore is as good as a Senior. It is with pleasure that I have seen their classmates showing disapproval of such actions, but the State feels that only by proper punishment visited by the Senior Class can they be brought to their senses.

"That their actions would readily lead to a complete revolt of the whole school, no sane nobleman or Senior could doubt. Tears come to my ears as I think of what may happen. Freshmen carrying canes. Sophomores spending some time in study and letting the team go to pot. Juniors learning to smoke hay-seed. Such are the horrors we may expect if we permit these ring-leaders to go on with their criminal actions.

"Your Dishonor, the State expects to prove that not only did these prisoners fly in the businesses called aeroplanes, but also say to reporters that they expected to discover the lost Atlantis in them, when all the world knows that Morgan Shuster discovered Atlantis, and hid it in the woodshed of the Headmaster at Yale, where it is to remain till a celebrated restaurant in Waterloo, Iowa, buys it for hash. Need I say more? Deliberately, these children, these—pardon the word—these brats, have set themselves up over Peary and Borup and Cap'n Scott. Talking to reporters! And them Sophomores! Sophomores!

"Furthermore, we shall prove by incompetent witnesses that they were seen last night trying to fly over to Mount Diablo in an aeroplane constructed of curtains swiped from the reception-room, with the Headmaster's coffee-percolator for an engine. Need I say more? (Shut up, Pink Eye, or I'll drool all night!)"

And Attorney Taffy Bingham sat down with great majesty. Gimlet Jones, for the prisoners, spoke shortly and to the point. Gimlet was noted for his eccentricity. If he had been expected to speak seriously, he would probably have made fun of the whole trial; but as he was expected to make fun of his clients, he said, very seriously:

"Your Honor, why doesn't this fool class do something original? Everybody expects us to kid these two Sophomores as much as we can. Why not admit that every last one of us is plain *jealous* of their bully flights? Why not admit, officially, what we all know, that Santa Benicia Academy has never even begun to have anything to be so proud of as it should be of these two fellows?"

There was silence all through the crowd as Gimlet sat down. In the wavering torch-light, the class looked considerably embarrassed. Then Taffy Bingham, champion wrestler, lost his head at what he considered spoiling their sport. He walked over to Hike, deliberately slapped Hike's face, and roared, "That's what I think of your blooming hero, Gimlet, you fool."

Hike stood up, very quick but very quiet. "You'll fight me for that, Taffy," he said, "and you'll get good and plenty licked. That wasn't part of the game. I'll punch you now or afterwards, whichever you want."

"Wait till afterwards," urged Gimlet, the only one besides Poodle who had heard Hike's low words.

"All right," said Hike, and sat down, while Taffy walked back to his place, white with passion.

Everybody pretended not to have seen the slap, and Taffy went on, as calmly as he could, to call the first witness. This witness was a new member of the Senior Class, who had spent the first three years of his prep. at San Dinero. Taffy explained that, as the new Senior knew nothing at all about the case, he would certainly be unprejudiced. Thus it went:

TAFFY: Did or did not the prisoners eat chocolate while 'planing to Mount Diablo with the reception-room curtains?

GIMLET: I object, Y'r Honor. Leading question.

JUDGE PINK EYE: 'Jection ov'ruled.

WITNESS: Yes, said the tomcat.

TAFFY: There, do you see? Now, witness, did or did not this Griffin wear spats when on Broadway?

PINK EYE (*sleepily*): 'Jection ov'ruled.

TAFFY: Shut up, you goat. Gwan, witness.

WITNESS: There should have been a fire-escape.

TAFFY: That's all right; beat it, witness. If Gimlet tries to cross-examine you, take the third turning to the right, beyond the ribbon counter. Your Dishonor, the State's case rests.

PINK EYE: Got any witnesses, Gimlet?

GIMLET: Taffy Bingham's witness enough for me.

PINK EYE: Guilty. Of—well, whatever it was they were charged—

GIMLET: Hey, hold on, Your Honor; we ain't summed up yet, and besides, we forgot to get a jury, in the first place.

THE CLASS (*with one voice*): Dry up, Gimlet. Let His Honor talk.

PINK EYE: Guilty, I said. I sentence them to a general hazing. First, they must get up before us and show us just how they run these cute little aeroplanes of theirs. Then, each of them must beat it around and beg the pardon of each member of the class, and not repeat themselves, either. Also, each Senior shall say something real cute and witty to 'em. But first, there's a Senior Class school edict, to be read by the school idiot—school crier, I mean. Let 'er go, Bunk.

BUNK TARVER: O yez, o yez, ten times. Listen, especially all youse Sophomores on the side lines (*Reads*): "This 'Trial and Punishment Extraordinary' will be enough to take it out of Griffin and Darby for having the cheek to get notorious; and *any one* that jollies them, after this, will get Senior Disfavor, also the Grand Queer. They're good fellows and good Santa Benicians and they are not to get kidded. This strictly goes. Signed by the whole Senior Class."

"Now for the aeroplane," shouted the Seniors. Chairs and sheets and golf sticks and a chafing dish and an automobile horn and a whole junk shop of other foolish things were handed into the center of the ring. Out of these, Hike and Poodle had to construct an aeroplane, and show how to fly it, while the Seniors let loose with all the insults of which, just then, they were able to think:

"How does the Army get along without you? How soon do you start teaching Captain Beck how to fly? When's Vedrines goin' to learn from you? Did you leave any air for the rest of us to fly in?"

When, finally, Hike and Poodle went solemnly around the Seniors and begged pardon of each for having dared to be born, the Hazing Extraordinary broke up joyously, with whoops and cheers—good, hearty, admiring cheers—for Hike and Poodle, in which the other classes joined. Most of the boys headed for their room and bedsteads.

Most—not all. Hike and Poodle, Taffy Bingham and Bunk Tarver of the Senior Class, and five others—two Sophomores and three Seniors—stood quietly waiting, under Fig Tree Major. When the Yard was quiet, and the lights had most of them gone out, Hike and Taffy quietly advanced into the center of the open space and shook hands.

Bunk Tarver, appointed referee, remarked, "As I get it, you two nuts want to fight because Taffy lost his head over Gimlet's renigging on the trial and slapped Griffin. Now, understand, there's to be no bad blood after this fight. This ends the whole thing, right now. One minute rounds and one minute rest between. No clinching. GO AHEAD!"

Just then happened the most surprising thing of all the many night fights that the wise old Fig Tree Major had seen beneath its crown.

Hike Griffin had been doing things rather different from the ordinary Santa Benicia ways, all summer. He had been working against and with a bunch of men who hit hard and quickly. So, instead of the timid circling with which an under-classman usually began a fight with a Senior, Hike waded in at once. No sparring—simply a quick right swing to the point of Taffy's jaw which jolted him terrifically. The wrestler, used to taking it more easily, made a foolish pat at the air, and got a rib-roaster for his pains. Then Hike bored in with a cruel blow he had learned in boxing with Jack Adeler. He swung for Taffy's jaw, apparently missed, and brought back his right with a back-hand which brought Taffy staggering to his knees, just as Bunk Tarver shouted "Time."

Taffy rose slowly, and Bunk declared, "Fight's over. No use going on with it. Griffin, you're all to the good. Taffy, old man, sorry, but you'll have to apologize."

Taffy started to growl a protest at the decision, but Bunk cut in, "I'm referee."

"That's right," declared Pink Eye Morrison.

"Well," Taffy rowed, "I ain't going to apologize—"

"Don't, old man," Hike astonished them all by saying. "*I'll* apologize. I know how it was—you forgot yourself; you weren't really intending to insult me. I'm sorry I got hot-headed over it; especially bein' 's I think these duel-fights are mostly foolish. Of course, if you want to fight on, I'm game; but I don't see any use of it. I'm sorry I started all the row, Bingham. Let's shake hands."

Still feeling very much jolted by Hike's backhander, still resentful at having been whipped, Taffy shook hands; and the group broke up.

"Gee, that was *great!*" Poodle caroled as he trotted back, beside Hike. "How you did lam—"

"Sorry I had to do it," growled Hike, most impolitely. "Fighting—like hoodlums. 'Course it's better than keeping ill-feeling going all year; but it's still better, strikes me, to wade into football, and that's what I'm going to do, to-morrow. I'm not goody-goody about the foolishness of fighting—I think it's a whole lot better than keeping up a grouch against a fellow. But when I think of men like General Thorne, that get along by keeping their tempers—why, that cute little scrap under Fig Tree Major looks awfully kiddish to me. But why I should be giving you a lecture on fighting, I don't know. How do you feel after the jamboree, old Poodski? Great idea of the Seniors, wasn't it? to end the kidding this way."

They were in their room, by this time, reflectively pulling off their clothes. "So you liked the idea of the hazing, did you?" Poodle asked.

"Why, sure. 'Course. Wonder who thought it up—probably Gimlet Jones."

"He *did* not," declared Poodle.

"How do you know? Who did get it up?"

"I did."

"*What?* You're crazy, Pood'."

"I planned it, and fixed it up with Pink Eye Morrison, and he got the Seniors to do it, as his idea. Why, *I even wrote that cutely insulting song they sang.* Sure, *I* had us hazed."

"Well I'll be—" began Hike, utterly amazed. Poodle retreated behind a chair, and picked up a shoe for defense.

"Well, what do you think of that?" was all Hike could say. "You got it all up. Say, young man, I don't know whether I ought to drop you out of the window or give you a prize."

"Let's compromise it, and get some sleep!" suggested Poodle.

CHAPTER XIX

AVIATING AGAIN!

THE coach of the Santa Benicia team was talking to Hike, after practise:

"Look here, Griffin, what's the trouble between you and the team? Looks to me as if they are still jealous of you for your aviating, and trying to show they're as good as you are. Breaks up team-play pretty badly. What have you got to suggest!"

"I don't know. I've been worrying over it. I'll see what I can do," said Hike, gloomily.

It was two weeks after the Great Hazing and now, though all the open "kidding" had stopped, there was still trouble. Hike was afraid that he might have to resign from the team, for the team's sake, though he would rather have cut off his head.

He wandered up to Lieutenant Adeler's room, worrying. He passed Sea Lion Rogers, who hailed him, "O Hike, got a minute!"

"No!" shouted Hike, and hurried on. Sea Lion Rogers was probably called that because he was so smooth that he could have slid through water like a seal. He was the son of a millionaire; he had traveled everywhere; he had manners like those of a duke in a play; and he always sneered. His chief amusement, these days, was to come up to Hike and ask some impossible question about aviation with the polished, courteous, smiling way which was more maddening than any "kidding." He was another thing that Hike had to settle—especially as some of the others were trying to imitate Rogers in this new sort of "kidding."

If he could only give the other members of the team a chance to aviate— well, *why couldn't he*?

It struck him as one of the finest little thoughts of the season, and he rushed into Jack Adeler's room cheerfully.

The Lieutenant looked up from a big book of electricity.

"Where can I get an aeroplane?" begged Hike. "I want one, right away."

"There isn't any other little thing you'd like, is there?"

"No, there isn't," stated Hike, refusing to be drawn. "I find the fellows keep thinking I'm an outsider, because of my aviating, and I want to bring a machine here, and get them into the feel of it."

"I see. Good idea. I've noticed you've been having trouble. It's made me pretty angry, but I thought I'd let you work it out. What do you want to do?"

"Why, I thought if I gave them some rides, it would make them feel they were aviators."

"They might. Worth trying, anyway. I'll tell you. A friend of mine has a Paulhan-Tatin monoplane, at Tanforan, just out of San Francisco. He's offered to lend it to me—wants me to regulate the motor and so on, I guess. We'll use that."

"When can we get it, Lieutenant?"

"To-night?"

"Great! That sounds like old times!"

The Lieutenant telephoned for the Santa Benicia town-hack, and to the Headmaster, and threw a toothbrush and a book into a suit-case, while Hike hurried off to pack his aviation-clothes. In half an hour they were on a train.

They found the Lieutenant's friend at his home on Pacific Avenue, San Francisco. The three climbed into a motor car, and whirled out to the aerodrome.

By the light of an electric lantern, Hike saw the Paulhan-Tatin monoplane, and gasped, for it looked like a fish, with funny wings, curved up at the ends; curved *up*; mind you. That, explained Jack Adeler, was for "automatic stability"—the bent wings kept the machine from tipping, without the aviator's having to warp (that is, bend up the edges of) the wings. The Paulhan was the latest thing in monoplanes, devised for the use of the French army. Its torpedo-shaped body cut through the air with the least head-resistance possible.

It sure was "different from the old *Hustle*," mused Hike. It could not even begin to carry so much weight, but it was faster, in comparison, for it made seventy to a hundred miles an hour with a forty horse-power motor, while the *Hustle* could only go two hundred to two hundred and fifty miles an hour, at the fastest, with two hundred and thirty horse-power.

"Seventy miles—that'll be fast enough for the fellows, I guess," laughed Hike.

He was shown just how the machine worked. He studied the new Gnome motor; the elevating planes—which were parts of a flat tail, at the back of the machine, instead of being separate planes in front. He sat in the aviator's cockpit, forward of the wings a little, and saw how the engine, though in front of him, worked a propeller, way back at the end of the tail.

While the Lieutenant was learnedly explaining that this fish-shaped body was in the "streamline form"—that is, the form best suited to pass through either air or water—Hike was wild to plunge out into the air again.

It didn't seem quite right to have just two long wings on the machine, instead of a whole nest of little tetrahedral planes all around him, but he liked this hot-headed, fiery little machine.

Half the night they spent in learning just how the machine worked; and next morning, the Lieutenant and the owner of it let him take it out on the aviation field for a little practise in speeding it along the ground, bobbing on its forward wheels, with its tail waggling in the air. Then he tried "grass cutting"—taking it up only a few feet.

The motor was of about the same sort as the *Hustle's* great Kulnoch, and by noon he felt that he could handle the machine in a respectable, honest wind that would not try to play tag with him. He said as much to Lieutenant Adeler, but that officer was as cautious as he was brave.

After lunch, at a country-club near the aerodrome, the three strolled back to the Paulhan-Tatin again. The mechanics wheeled it out of its aerodrome. Hike crawled into it, and sat there, idly.

Suddenly there was the buzz of a motor starting, and a Modified Jolls Bi-plane ran along its course and launched up, headed for the south, disappearing in a few moments, as though it were enjoying itself. The sun flashed on its cloth surfaces. It seemed to be part of the blue sky. It was too much for Hike.

"Start the motor—give the propeller a couple of whirls, will you!" Hike muttered to a mechanic, and an instant later he was hurtling down the field, at full speed, then jumping off the ground. He soared up—up—up—then turned, in a graceful circle, passed over the hangars, and headed north—toward Santa Benicia.

Up in the air again—oh! it was *great*! He felt as though he ought to come down and ask the Lieutenant's permission before really taking a trip, but—this was so good! The cracking motor sounded sweeter to him than any music he had ever heard. He whooped as he faced the fresh breeze from the Pacific—and then he settled calmly down to reaching Santa Benicia Academy as soon as he could.

It was forty miles away, and he was flying at eighty miles an hour. The slender, fishy body cut through air like a shark churning foam. He had to make a curve around San Francisco, but nevertheless he sighted the towers of the academy in thirty-five minutes after he had left Tanforan—and it seemed like five minutes.

He was careful. ("Sure I'm careful!" he apologized to himself.) He had to watch out for the differences in control between the monoplane and the tetrahedral—the elevating planes were at the opposite end, and worked oppositely, for instance.

But careful or not, he was so excited over speeding again that he had to yell "Wow, WOW!" about every three minutes, to relieve his nerves. He'd never lose his love for the *Hustle*. No other machine could load enough gasoline to speed across the country, and carry a large enough motor to make two hundred an hour. But this—this was like riding on a bow of a torpedo-boat going at forty knots, while driving the *Hustle* was like strolling along the decks of a big liner, easier but not half so exciting. So Hike whooped and sang, in the cockpit, close to the wings, and hurled the Paulhan-Tatin at Santa Benicia.

He circled all about the campus twice, then darted down in the Yard, landing at sixty miles an hour—like a bullet striking a steel plate and glancing off. He shot across the long grass plot, with the body of the machine bumping and leaping up into the air, as it bounced on the tires of its wheels. The tail flapped as though the whole machine was going to turn over. It looked as if the nose would smash into the archway, at the end of the Yard. It stopped only a few feet away.

Hike looked slightly scared, as he crawled out of the cockpit. "Gee! That's different from landing in the *Hustle*!" he admitted. "I didn't think even a monoplane would come down quite that fast!"

The whole academy came rushing up. "Old Grouch," the Greek master, who was holding a recitation in Anabasis, actually dismissed the class, and came running out, with a piece of chalk still in one hand.

The football-team had just been starting for the athletic-field, in twos and threes. Though the coach yelled at them, they deserted the field and came tearing into the Yard.

"Hey, you footballers—come on and have a ride!" shouted Hike, and climbed back into the cockpit of the monoplane. From this elevation, he saw Taffy Bingham on the edge of the crowd. "Come on, Taffy," he added, but Taffy shook his head, rather scornfully, and strolled away.

However, eight members of the eleven, with a dozen subs., gathered nearest the machine, while the crowd regretfully made way for them. Even the glory of their football suits, and school sweaters, was dimmed as they gazed at Hike's Balaclava helmet and leather jacket. They looked as though they wanted a ride, yet didn't want to show themselves inferior to this aviator.

"Say, fellows," pleaded Hike, "I wanted you all to have a share in this blooming aviation business, and I brought up this machine for you. Won't you ride with me. I know just as well as you do that the only reason I've ever done any aviating is just because I've had the chance, and I want to get you in on it."

Over the faces of the crowd spread a look of great love for Hike, as they heard him and privately assured themselves that undoubtedly they would be great aviators, too, if they had the chance.

"Gee, that's awfully good of you, old Hike!" said Pink Eye Morrison—and he didn't talk like a Senior addressing a Sophomore, either!

"Help me wheel the machine out on the field, where there's more room," said Hike, and as many hands as could find place on the machine started her off before Hike had time to climb out of the cockpit.

He had Pink Eye climb in behind him, when they reached the field. It took the rest of the team to clear away the crowd that insisted on gathering right in front of the machine.

Hike started away at the slowest speed he could manage, but the Paulhan shot into the air like an arrow. He wished that he had the easy-going *Hustle*. He glanced back and saw Pink Eye trying to smile, but catching his breath and gasping. Hike grabbed the hand-throttle and slowed down as best he could.

He took the machine on a long, level course, over the safest country he could find—the sweep of tules in the marshes along the straits; and when he reached the athletic field, he brought her down as easily as possible. But even so, Pink Eye was pale and limp when he climbed out.

"Great work," exclaimed Hike, before Pink Eye could say a word. "You took to the air great. You're an aviator already."

"Did I take it all right?" asked Pink Eye gratefully, enjoying the glances of envy from the crowd. "Thanks a hundred times, old Hike."

And Hike knew that there was one member of the team, at least, who would not bother him by envy any longer.

Pink Eye was already explaining to his team-mates how much he had enjoyed the ride, and stating at length that the view of the tules, as seen from a monoplane at about seventy miles an hour, is very fine indeed. But the others were not very anxious to ride; not after having seen the monoplane come swooping down and hit the earth at over fifty miles an hour. Even Bill McDever, the captain—stolid Bill who never said much, and wasn't much known, but was always the center of team-plays—seemed a little agitated, when he crawled in, as the next passenger.

Half of the team, didn't want to ride, much, but they felt that they had to, or never be seen in those parts again! As each got out, there was the same hearty hand-shake from Hike, and the same thankful affection given Hike by his team-mates.

Perhaps it was because they were so surprised and delighted to get back alive, after roaring through the air, bumping on air-currents, and seeing houses look like dice beneath them, that they loved Hike exceedingly when they landed; or perhaps it was because they felt he wanted them to share in his glory, or because they respected him to the limit when they saw how he could run the dragon through the air as though he were riding a bicycle. Perhaps it was all three.

By late afternoon, Hike had given short trips to all of the team and subs. that were in sight. It was Football Day in aviation. Practise was called off. But he had to refuse the others—he even took Poodle for only a five-minute spin. However, there was one Sophomore whom he very much wanted to treat, and that was his dear, courteous friend Sea Lion Rogers (sometimes known as "Slimy" Rogers).

He had twice noticed Sea Lion, standing on the edge of the crowd, with his usual polite sneer. He whispered to Morrison, "Say Pink Eye, you know how Slimy Rogers has been kidding me? Would you mind getting him to come up and ask me a fool question—let him think you want to have me kidded. Then I'll give him a happy little ride. Oh, thanks."

Hike managed to look very much surprised when, after giving the last sub. a ride, he found Sea Lion edging up to the machine, and asking, in loud cheerful tones for the crowd to hear, "Oh say, Griffin, can you tell me what the angle of incidence is in this Poling-Tating machine?"

"Jump in and I'll show you, Sea Lion," said Hike cheerfully.

The polished youth drew back, and stammered, "Why, I thought you said you'd only have time to take the team, and Poodle, for a ride. I don't want to butt in—thanks just the same, but there's a couple of the team—Taffy, anyway,—that haven't ridden yet. Much obliged, just the same. I wish I could ride with you."

"Why, I didn't say nothing about your *riding*, I just wanted you to see how the aviator's seat was fixed," said Hike innocently.

Sea Lion looked foolish. The crowd began to grin, in sympathy with Hike. They crowded closer, till the machine was like the lion's cage at the country circus.

"But, Sea Lion," went on Hike, "since you make me think of it, I don't know but what I will take you for a little spin. You see, there isn't anybody in the school who's so much interested in aviation as you are—I can tell that by the number of questions you ask."

The crowd howled, for many of them had heard Sea Lion's tormenting questions.

"Get in, Sea Lion; get in, Slimy; you aren't scared, are you?" they yelled at him, and lifted him bodily, till he fairly had to get into the cockpit.

Hike had been standing up, gently smiling, with his helmet pushed back on his damp locks, and his goggles hanging below his chin. He snapped back the goggles, and fastened down the helmet, sharply. He crouched in the pit, yelling, "Out of the road—quick—look out!" Poodle spun the propeller.

As the crowd scattered, the monoplane ran down the field like a runaway locomotive. It shot out straight across the trees, at the edge of the field, at top speed, eighty miles an hour. Hike's heart thumped horribly, for a tenth of a second, as the wheels on the chassis just grazed the tree-tops, and the whole machine threatened to crash down.

Sea Lion, behind him, nearly fainted.

Hike took her up, way up. He ascended in great circles, till he was up two thousand feet, then scooted down, in a straight line, aiming for the center of the Carquinez Straits. It looked as if they were going to hit the river-bottom, and never come up.

He came so near to the water that one wing scattered spray, as he steered her up. He circled quickly, and headed across the town for the campus again. He dipped down, as though he were going to stop. He glanced back. On Sea Lion's pale face was a look of relief that could not be described.

"Poor boy, he thinks this is all," reflected Hike, as he darted away. In what seemed like a second, they were buzzing over the hills that surrounded Santa Benicia. The gusts from between peaks rocked them till sometimes they seemed to be in a small boat on a rough sea.

Then he flew to the academy again. He rounded the flag-pole, a lofty redwood on the athletic field. As he rounded it, he banked so sharply that the right wing stood almost straight up, and the left down.

The crowd below howled with terror. They thought the machine was falling, going to land on its side, wing-first.

But it suddenly straightened up. Hike shot her almost straight down to earth, within few feet of the ground; then way up, then sharply down again, in the "Dutch roll."

As he swooped down the second time, he looked back at Sea Lion. The Class Tease was clinching his teeth till the edges of his mouth stood out in huge wrinkles while his open lips made tight, hard lines across his teeth. His eyes were closed. He was clutching the edge of the cockpit with both hands.

This was quite too much triumph for Hike. He felt very sorry for Sea Lion as he circled again, and landed. He felt still sorrier as Sea Lion was lifted out, and staggered off, silent, while all his acquaintances yelled at him, "What did you find was the bangle of accidence, Slimy?"

"Good-by," cried Hike, and started for Tanforan. He knew that there would be no more "kidding," and mighty little more jealousy, the rest of the year.

CHAPTER XX

THE GAME WITH THE ETONIANS

MOST of the California schools and colleges play Rugby football, like the English and the Australians. But a good many schools which prepare students for eastern colleges still play the American game, and among these are Santa Benicia, Hike's school; the great San Dinero Preparatory School, where the sons of millionaires learn polo and (say the Santa Benicians) brush their teeth with gold brushes; and the Berkeley Etonian School.

The Etonians were not very dangerous, but the Santa Benicians liked to make a good meal on them, about October, to whet their teeth for Dumnor High School, and the big San Dinero game. In the game with the Etonians, the team assumes what is likely to be its final shape; so all the friends of the players come out with yells concealed in their throats, to cheer particular friends.

Poodle Darby, wearing a large and gaudy sweater, was very conspicuous on the home-ground bleachers, as the crowd flocked in for the Etonian game. He was explaining that, as Hike had been not only captain and right-half, on the Freshman team of the year before, but also easily the best player, Hike was certain to make good in the position of left-half on the school team, in which he was to be finally tried out at this game.

In the dressing room, Hike was putting on his shin-guards, singing. He was not nervous. Though he was anxious lest the coach or captain might take him out of the game, he was mad with desire to get into a scrimmage —or to be flying swiftly, in the *Hustle*, against a head wind; he didn't much care which. It seemed advisable, first, however, to attend to the Etonians. He paid little attention to the knot about Poodle, which cheered him as he came out on the field. He merely started getting up steam by passing the ball.

When the team ran up against the Etonians after about the first down, they had the surprise of their lives. This time, they were not facing one of the mobs of half-sized boys which the Etonians usually called a team, but a sturdy bunch with play like clock-work and a grit that made up for their lack of weight. The Santa Benicians tried again and again to rush the ball through the line, but the Etonians hung on like bull-pups.

Once, Hike got clear with the ball, but he was tackled by two Etonians and came down in ten yards. Once, Bunk Tarver, at right-end, recovered an onside kick, just at the end of the first half, and made the only touch-down of the first half. Snifty Carter missed his goal-kick. The Santa Benicians on the bleachers cheered only half-heartedly. Where were the brilliant team-plays, the forward passes, the long runs, and the magnificent punts which they expected to see brought out of cover during this game? Where, oh, where?

And the coach, a Princeton crack, asked the same; only he asked it over and over, making most uncomplimentary references to a "bunch of butter-fingered dough-heads," as he addressed the team between the halves. He warned Taffy Bingham, the right-tackle, that he was playing carelessly, and that the line would get a hole bored in it, unless he watched out. Taffy deliberately turned his back and paid little attention. The coach, who hated Taffy's sneers, longed to be able to put some one else in his place, but had no one so good.

Early in the second half, Taffy was playing more carelessly than ever, though Bill McDever, captain of the team, and right-guard, used terrific language to him. And just then the Etonians got through, brushed Taffy aside, tossed on a trick, and landed a touch-down. Furthermore, they kicked goal successfully—and now their score was ahead of the Santa Benicians.

Poodle was biting the front of the seat above him, and kicking as though dying of three or four diseases at once, while the hundred rooters that the Etonians had brought danced all over each other.

Then the Etonians held the Santa Benicians down for fifteen terrible minutes, till Hike, Hike Griffin, got around left end on a fake kick, and made a forty-yard run, while the whole school gasped, afraid to breathe. A fast little Etonian, caught at him as he passed, but he shook the sprinter off with a laugh, and loped ahead. The breeze hit his face; he made b'lieve—just plain made b'lieve—that he was driving the *Hustle* before Congress and the President; gritted his teeth, and fled toward the Etonian goal. As he reached a clear field, the Santa Benicians all rose and bawled, "Hike, Hike, hike; hike, Hike, hike!" He hiked.

He made that touch-down. Captain Bill McDever reached him, pounded him on the back, and grinned, asking cheerfully, "What were you running so fast for? Nobody near you. Save your wind." Poodle had sneaked into the field. He got there just in time to explain. "Hike forgot his handkerchief and went back to get it," before he was ordered off the field.

Then, to add to the general joy, Snifty Carter kicked goal, safely.

For the rest of the game, not another score was made. But the game was won for Santa Benicia and—but let Poodle explain—"and Hike had that job as right-half cinched for the rest of his life, with a raise every week!"

The team was stripping off sweaters and socks, when Taffy Bingham came up to Hike.

"Griffin," he said, "that was a great run you made. And it was my bum playing that made it necessary. You made me want to buck up and—Shake hands, Griffin—uh—*Hike*, old man!"

The coach said nothing, but he was very glad, because he knew that this meant all the bad blood between Hike and Taffy had flowed by.

And Hike rejoiced, because he hated to have any one hate him. Also, he now realized that he must have made a good run. He had been too busy to think much about it. Timidly, he approached the coach and asked, "Do you think I'll have a chance to stick on the team, now?"

"Well, if you don't put some *form* into your running, and quit thinking about chewing gum and aviating when you ought to get into the game, we'll use you for taking tickets," growled the coach.

As that was all he said, Hike rejoiced, for he knew that he was practically safe for three years of playing! Otherwise the coach would have eaten him at one bite.

Lieutenant Jack Adeler was reading, that evening, amid a confusion of diagrams of wireless instruments, and plans of motors, when Mousey Tincom and four other Sophomores knocked.

"Please, sir, Lieutenant Adeler," begged Mousey, "we heard that you'll give out the list of Soph. corporals to-morrow, and that Griffin may be left out, because you were afraid it would look—not look right—if you appointed—Hike, being a personal friend of yours—Please, sir, we don't want to butt in, but the whole class, honest, sir—"

"Does the whole class really want him?" queried Lieutenant Adeler.

"Yes, sir."

"All right. I understand."

Next day when the military appointments were announced, Hike's name was among the corporals. And the only complaint the school made was that Hike was not first sergeant.

CHAPTER XXI

LEFT EARED DONGAN

LEFT EARED DONGAN, Sophomore, jester of the Fig Tree Celebration and candidate for football-end, was not a Great Man, just then. He was an aeroplane. It may have looked as though he was merely a boy, running over a hilltop, two miles from the academy, waving his arms madly. But that was a mistake. Not only was he really an Updegraff monoplane, but also he was breaking all records. Of course he was alone. He would not, for his chances of becoming end, have allowed any one to see him making b'lieve.

He twisted the second button on his coat; which, as every aviator knows, steers an aeroplane (that is, when the aeroplane is a Santa Benicia Sophomore). Then he pulled his nose, which turns down the elevating planes, and puffed up the last stretch of Bilbunet Hill.

He saw a bunch of chaparral, and suddenly he was not an aeroplane. Not at all. He was Colonel Church, leading a brilliant night attack on Yaqui Indians. But his trousers got fuzzy, and he became an aeroplane again.

He soared through a little pass, toward a deserted shack once occupied by a shepherd, away from all the regular hill-paths. He sat down with his back against the board walls, trying to work out the following terrific problem:

If your arms are the wings of an aeroplane, how can you use the hands that are so inconveniently stuck way out there at the end of those arms, to manage levers?

He was just deciding that, perhaps, after all, according to the practise of the best aeroplane-builders, coat-tails, and not arms, are planes, when he heard a sound within the cabin.

He was startled. There was a mumbling, kept up for some time, and accompanied by a low pounding on wood.

Left Ear promptly became Sherlock Holmes. Dragging Dr. Watson along, he sneaked about to the back of the cabin and looked in through a little window.

There stood Poodle Darby, by a wooden kitchen-table, reading aloud from a sheet of paper, and keeping time by tapping on the table!

The room was bare, except for the table, a chair, and many papers.

Left Ear gleefully chortled to himself. "So *here's* where you come when you want to write poetry for the school mag., is it, Mr. Poodle? You think you *will* keep us away, do you? You think you will get in poetries on us, do you?"

By this time he was running down the hill side, too busy even to be an aeroplane.

He gathered the first four Sophomores whom he met in the Yard, explained to them in a gasping yelp the awful thing Poodle was doing, and the five started on the dogtrot for the shack on Bilbunet Hill.

As they edged up to the window, Poodle was in the midst of reading the poem all over again, after having rewritten a couple of lines. He read it loudly and clearly. He must have liked it, for the joyous listeners outside heard him declare, "Say, that ain't *half* bad!"

"Sure it ain't!" shouted Left Ear, outside, and the five rushed for the open door on the other side of the shack.

Poodle arose, in huge horror, and faced five large, happy grins.

"We thought we'd call on you and read you some of our poetry," said Left Ear. "It's so nice (ain't it? Yes, no? sure it is, little Poodle; now don't you answer me back) to have a fellow-goat—excuse me, fellow-poet, I meant—sympathize with you, in this crool world. Say, will you fellows just sit on Poodle," he suggested to the other four, "and I'll read you some of the beau-ti-ful things he has on that mahogany kitchen-table there. Oh, Poodle, how *could* you be so crool and keep them gems from us?"

There is an unwritten law of Santa Benicia that when a man is about to be subjected to a "jolly," he may, if he have reasonable excuse, state it, and not receive the "jolly," yet not be regarded as "begging off." However, if he attempt to do this very often, it will take an excuse that would shake the world to be accepted as good. Poodle had never tried to get out of being "jollied" before, but this time he pleaded.

"Aw don't Left Eared.... *Reason'ble 'Scuse!* This stuff I'm writing is for the school paper—it's verse, all righto, but you'll spoil it for me if you read it."

"It don't go—bum excuse," growled Left Ear, furious at the prospect of losing this chance of being in the lime-light.

"It *does* go—first time I ever made Reason'ble 'Scuse; and it *is* reasonable, and it's going to go."

"Nix," chortled the others, hypnotized by Left Ear. But they were suddenly surprised and shocked to see Poodle, with one quick motion, upset the table and chair, in a corner, and spring behind it, where he doubled up his fists and got into an attitude of defense. They edged toward him.

Left Ear stooped to pick up a paper fallen from the table in front of the barricade. But he caught, instead of the paper, Poodle's fist under his chin. He was slightly lifted up, and dropped hard, on the floor.

Just then, the five saw Poodle violently shake his head and remark "I'll handle 'em," as if to some one *behind* them. They turned, to see Hike standing at the door, leaning against the door-jambs carelessly, and smiling very sweetly. Said Hike:

"Well, speeds, having a pleasant little time with yourself? You know the law that if you don't accept a *really* Reason'ble 'Scuse, then the victim is expected to fight, and his friends can help him, don't you? I got here about the same time you did, and it strikes me that what Poodle said was Reason'ble 'Scuse, all right. You'll spoil his stuff for him if you monkey with it before he hands it into the paper. You know mighty well and *good*" (Hike, as he talked, was getting angry), "that this is the first time Pood' ever made *any* excuse to keep from being jollied, and so—"

He stepped in, like a panther, quick, silent, and grabbed the first classmate by the collar, and threw him clean through the door. The others, except Left Ear, chorused, "You're right, Hike—we got excited, I guess. We'll fight if you want to, but we admit we're in bad."

"All right," said Hike. "How about you, Left Ear? By the way, you know you didn't have any right to butt in here—this ain't on the school grounds; it's Poodle's private Country Estate, and you've got no right to come in here unless he invites you—especially if he wants to sport his oak. And he doesn't invite anybody—even me—very often. You goats keep him from writing down there, and if he wants to write up here, it's his privilege. I understand it was you that led this business—I heard down in the Yard how you came rushing down there to get the gang."

Now, Mr. Left Ear Dongan was not a bad chap, but he was as thoughtless as a runaway engine with a dead engineer. He had been badly jolted by Poodle's fist, and his merry game was spoiled, so he snarled:

"All right. If Poodle's such a big baby that he can't stand for a little kidding, why we'll give him a milk-bottle and let him sneak out here and have a good time with himself. And talk about butting in—I'd like to know what else *you're* doing—coming here and talking like you was a big brother, or a faculty member. 'Especially if he wants to sport his oak.' You must think you're in Oxford. I suppose you think you're aviating with— You and your baby brother, here. Oh, piffle!"

Hike laughed, "You've got sand, anyway, Lefty. You know I can lick you, without trying. But don't splutter so much; we can't catch what you say. By the way, 'like you was' strikes me as rotten grammar—and I ain't any too careful myself."

"You sure ain't," snarled Left Ear. "'Ain't' is about as ungrammatical as anything I could ever say." He wondered why the rest of the gang grinned, when he looked to them for approval and comfort.

"Right you are, Lefty," hummed Hike, and continued, "Now, about Poodle's being a baby. How about that, Pood'?"

"No," said Poodle, shortly. "Fight. To-night. Fig Tree Major. Heh, Left Eared?"

"All right," said Left Ear, and departed, still furious.

"Sorry you've got to fight—don't like it much, even if I did fight with Taffy, t'other day," mused Hike. "But I guess it'll be the only way to calm down Left Ear. He'll be a good friend of ours, after you beat him up."

Hike knew, and Poodle knew, that Poodle was not at all likely to do anything like "beating up" Left Ear, who was certain to stand high in the school boxing-contest, as well as to make the football-team, one of these days.

In a way, Poodle had more courage than Hike—he was not half so strong, yet he was no more afraid.

It showed that night in the way in which he faced Left Ear, and took a bloody nose without flinching.

"There," cried Hike to Poodle, as they returned home after the fight. "I hope that will be the last nose-punching we'll have to go through with. It's too kiddish, that's all."

But he knew that Left Eared Dongan was still angry, and that he would have to discover some way of soothing that imaginative person. How—when? He didn't know. But he'd have to find the way. Meanwhile (as he continued to Poodle):

"I'm going to cut out *all* this strong-arm business, aeroplaning and everything else, just as soon as football-season is over. I'm going to settle down right now, and study electricity, all the time. Study! Nobody'll get me out of my room, not for one minute, except for recitations and football. Me for the quiet life. No fighting, no aeroplaning, no nothing, till—"

Just then Poodle pounced on a yellow envelope which had been poked under their door while they were away. "Telegram for you, Hike," he said.

Hike read it over, then exclaimed, "Well, what do you think of that! Cap'n Wibbelty-Wobbelty's on the loose! Well, what *do* you think of *that*?"

"We'd all be glad to tell you what we think of it before we hear it," said Poodle.

"Oh, pardon *me*. Here she is. Want the address read, too?"

"Oh, Hike, *please* read it, if it's got anything to do with Wibbelty-Wobbelty."

"Listen:

'Come to San Francisco at once. Meet me Palace Hotel. Captain Welch in Mexico making trouble at my ranch. Insurrectos. Need help with tetrahedral. Explain when come. Hurry.

'John Adeler.'"

"Wow!" said Poodle, amazed, and—

"Wow!" roared Hike, in a different tone, wildly excited. "This means a hike on the *Hustle*. Mexico—insurrectos—night flight—wow!" He grabbed his cap, tossed a time-table to Poodle, and cried, "Please, Pood', see what's the next train I get into town. I'm going to see the Headmaster right now, and get leave to—"

"See him at midnight?" howled Poodle. "And permit us to *state* that there ain't any trains between midnight and dawn."

"Gee, that's so," mourned Hike. "I was so excited I forgot it was late at all."

"Yes," remarked Poodle. "You were some excited. This is that 'no aero-planing, no nothing' that we were just hearing about, ain't it?"

"Uh-huh. Gee, Poodle, I'm just *crazy* over this. Gee, it's great.... Out in the *Hustle*. Mexico. Cap'n Welch. It's too good to be true!"

CHAPTER XXII

TROUBLE IN MEXICO

LIEUTENANT JACK ADELER, dressed in riding breeches and khaki Norfolk jacket, was pacing the lobby of the Palace Hotel, waiting. As he saw a tall youngster enter the revolving door, he hastened to him and, with not a word, dragged him off to his private room.

"Hike," Jack Adeler exclaimed, "can you get away for two weeks, and come with me to Mexico, to drive the *Hustle*, and fight off some insurrectos? They're attacking my rancho, down there. I can get leave from the Headmaster for you—I telegraphed him. But what about football?"

Hike thought quickly. "Well, I'll have to miss a couple of games. They can put in Left Eared Dongan and—"

"So *that's* what you call Dongan," smiled the Lieutenant, hurried though he was.

"Sure. Pink Eye Morrison chewed his left ear for calling him 'Glass Arm' once!... Well, I can get back in time for the last two games— You're sure we won't take over two weeks?"

"Not much over, certainly."

"Well, anyway, I can get back in time for the big Thanksgiving game with San Dinero."

"All right; that's settled, then. Now, listen." And Jack Adeler explained the "why" of this jaunt to Mexico:

"Captain Welch has turned up again—like the bad penny. He's in Lower California—that's a province of Mexico, you know. There isn't supposed to be any more revolution in Mexico, now, but believe me when I say that there's *always* more or less revolution in Lower California. That part of Mexico is more or less shut off from the rest, with some pretty savage islands on the west. I believe there's a real tribe of cannibal Indians, near Tiburon Isle.

"Well, Captain Welch has turned up there as a Colonel commanding a tough regiment of Mexicans, Indians, and rascally Americans. They are simply robbing and plundering, and calling it 'revolution.' The authorities in that part of the state can't do a thing with them. Well, they are heading for my rancho, at Aguas Grandes—which means there's a two-by-four creek running through the desert, and they call it 'Aguas Grandes,'—big waters.

"My foreman has telegraphed me that he knows Welch is going to attack, though Welch is taking his time getting there, plundering on the way. If we get there by midnight, to-morrow night, we'll probably be in time.

"We'll just have to fight. Welch has got the authorities so scared that they're more likely to help him than to protect the rancheros. Martin Priest is coming with a tetrahedral—with the *Hustle*—and you and I will take that —it ought to be here by four this afternoon—and cart a machine-gun down to my rancho, and be ready for Welch. Is it a go?"

"Sure. Four this afternoon? I'll rush out to Santa Benicia for clothes and a revolver, and be back here before then. Oh, say, is Poodle in on this? Aw, please, please take him. He'll be all broke up if he doesn't get taken."

"I'm sorry—I wish we could; but it's impossible. He's a corking boy, but scarcely enough of a fighter for this—though, of course, he's got plenty of courage."

Hike believed the Lieutenant wrong. He remembered how Poodle had stood up to Left Ear, showing enough courage in this schoolboy-fight to take him into a real battle, even with insurrectos. But the Lieutenant was his commander, and he merely saluted.

"By the way, Hike, don't even mention this. Just let the Headmaster and Poodle know where you're going. They'll keep still. I had to confide in the Headmaster myself. Be sure about this, for remember that if this got into the newspapers, it might mean big international trouble between the United States and Mexico—an American army officer fighting on Mexican territory. I'm going as a private citizen, a ranchero, and I don't want any one to know I'm anything else."

"Right O!" promised Hike, and hurried out for the next train to Santa Benicia, wild with the joy of going, and feeling (it must be confessed) rather important, thus entrusted with a secret which could make trouble between two nations.

* * * *

At Santa Benicia, Hike had two hard tasks that he had to get through quickly, and one that was a joy. This last was the packing of his aviating garments—his paper gloves, of a soft French paper, for warmth; his Balaclava aviator's helmet; muffler, overalls, aluminoid-silk Flying Jacket; together with his revolver, water-bottle, and emergency box of capsules of food—with which, a flat pilly-looking lozenge made fair soup for a hungry and stranded aviator. He loved the things, for they meant flight and adventure.

But he had those other two tasks. He had to tell Poodle that he couldn't go along. Poodle was hard hit, though he pretended that he wasn't, busily helping Hike pack.

Then Hike had to tell the captain of the team, Bill McDever, that he was called away for two weeks. McDever was a kindly, quiet chap, who adored Santa Benicia Academy as much as he hated any one who was unclean of mouth and didn't take exercise. McDever pleaded with Hike; he spoke of Santa Benicia's need. Hike loved Santa Benicia, but there was an even louder call to duty—that of Jack Adeler and the endangered rancheros, and the tetrahedral. So he had to say, "No, sorry, McDever—I've got to go."

Then the captain half threatened and half warned him with something that Hike hadn't thought of. "If you go off this way, old man, you'll smash training up so badly, that there'll be horribly little chance of your getting into the San Dinero game. I don't want that to happen, either for your sake or for the sake of the team."

"Gee, that's so," mourned Hike. "I might be in pretty bad trim for the game. But even so, I'm afraid I have to go. There's—there's a big duty."

"I believe you," said McDever, heartily, "and good luck to you, anyway. Get back as soon as you can; and I *hope* that even if you *are* away two weeks, it may not be necessary to drop you from the line-up."

Hike hoped so, too. But, anyway, he made himself simply forget the question of whether he would lose his chance on the team or not, and faced Mexico and the battle.

CHAPTER XXIII

REBELS AT THE BORDER

NIGHT on the desert. There seemed to be millions of new stars in the sky, as they whirred over the dead world of sand and cactus, in the *Hustle*. The Lieutenant was taking a nap, nestling in a long cloak, between the Benet-Mercier machine-gun and a pile of cartridge-boxes. Hike was driving the tetrahedral, glad to be facing the winds again, glad to be shooting ahead at nearly a hundred miles an hour, instead of dawdling across the Yard. But he was a little anxious, too, for he was afraid that he was lost.

He kept searching the roller-map, in front of him. There were so few landmarks. He had no towns, with brilliant arc lights, to go by. He wanted to ask the Lieutenant's opinion of where they were, but also he didn't want to wake the tired man. He took the chance that they were near the spot where the corners of Arizona and California nearly meet, on the border of Mexico, and turned southwestward.

Far off, there was a tiny, broad-spread glow on the clouds. Could that be a desert village? But why lights so late at night? In any case, he was going to find out.

There seemed to be nothing in the world, as he soared, except the stars, brilliant overhead, the rushing aeroplane, and that glow ahead. The glow departed, and he studied what looked like a big camp-fire. It *was* a camp-fire, he found out, a minute later. He circled it, quietly, with the motor and lights shut off, noting the men passing about it. One stood out clearly in the full red flare of the flames, looking into the fire, unconscious of the tetrahedral 'planing above him. Hike peered at the man carefully, for the sudden fear had come, "Suppose this should be a camp of revolutionists? Suppose we're already in the region of the revolution?"

But the man was not in uniform. He seemed to be an American, a cow-puncher, in overalls, a sombrero, and a flannel shirt. Again, easily, softly, slowly—much more slowly than any aeroplane except the tetrahedral could have done—he circled the fire, trying to make out what sort of men were those sleeping about the fire. He could not tell. But he saw an open space, beyond the bunch of picketed horses, and dropped the *Hustle* safely in the space.

The horses set up a frightened neighing. Instantly, the man by the fire shouted something in Mexican, and two hundred men sprang out of their blankets and rushed toward Hike and the tetrahedral. In the dim light there, some distance from the fire, he saw that they all carried guns—carbines, shotguns, modern rifles—even some Krags and Parsley-Chardon repeaters; and about half of them were in some sort of uniforms; here an American army khaki shirt, here a French military cap, here a pair of shabby shoulder-straps.

So he had fallen among the revolutionists!

He started to snap on the motor, but an insurrecto sprang up beside him and caught his arm. Even then, Hike's first thought was for the safety of Lieutenant Adeler and the machine-gun. With one quick twist of his head, he saw that the Lieutenant, though still wobbly after his quick awakening from sleep, had managed to throw a tarpaulin over the gun and cartridges, and that he was concealed from the revolutionists behind that black covering.

"Leggo my arm!" Hike snapped at the insurrecto.

From the midst of the group rushed the man who had been standing by the fire. Now that he was so close, Hike could see that he had, pinned on a shoulder, one shoulder-strap, with the insignium of a major. It was all there was of his uniform!

The man shouted something in Mexican again, and added in English, "Let him alone, you-all." He talked like a Virginian, with a soft, mellow, sweet voice, that sounded as though it could get very angry. "We can use him and his flying machine, Ah reckon!"

Then Hike realized that many of these revolutionists were Americans. Some looked like tough horse-thieves, some like adventurous young chaps from ranches. And with that came the sharp thought, "What if Welch were in this bunch?" That suggested what he ought to do.

"Major," he cried, "I'm under Colonel Welch's orders, and I'm bringing him a—a—bringing his despatches. I want to get my directions, and what you know about his present location."

The "Major" seemed startled. "Welch? You with him?"

"I sure am," declared Hike, wishing that he soon might be "with" him, at least.

The ruse worked. But before the "Major" answered Hike, he spoke with a Mexican who had quantities of gold lace over a shabby weather-worn old uniform-coat.

Just then Jack Adeler's head bobbed up from behind the tarpaulin-covered gun and cartridges at the back. Hike, looking back, felt very anxious. What had he been doing back there? Could it be that Jack Adeler—*Jack Adeler!*—was afraid of a bunch of plundering bush-fighters? If the machine-gun were only loaded—what they could do—!

He heard the Lieutenant whispering sharply, "Find out where we are."

"Where are we?" he blurted out to the "Major."

"Ten miles southeast of Calientado—seventeen miles from the border.... But say, Ah don't think we'd better let you-all go yet. Ah'll have to see your despatches, first, and then, if they're all right, Ah'll have Captain Grendez here go—"

Suddenly Jack Adeler's voice bellowed from the freight-platform, "Stand aside, there, all of you, or we'll shoot you." He was waving a revolver with one hand and jerking at the tarpaulin cover with the other.

The "Major" seemed only quietly amused. "Ah *thought* what you said was only a ruse," he laughed. "You, back there, you better put up that pop-gun or you might hurt yourself, 'cause when we—"

Just then the tarpaulin came off. Jack Adeler turned a handle, and the machine-gun went "trrrrrrr," like an automobile racing without a muffler.

Ten men about the machine toppled over, and the rest fled terrified, throwing away their guns as they ran, scattering into the darkness, bellowing horrified fear.

Instantly, Hike switched on the contact. The *Hustle* bumped along the soft ground, stuck a moment in the sand, then went up at a long slant, dangerously close to the fire. In a second she was running smooth, as though on cushions of eiderdown. Jack Adeler, stopping only to cover the machine-gun, came down to the passenger seat beside Hike.

Hike's nerves had been terrible shaken by the sight of men falling over, struck by the hurricane of shells from the machine-gun; and it was all he could do to keep his levers on the jiggle. His nerve was fairly gone, for once.

Through the crack of the motor, he shouted to the Lieutenant, "I hope *they* weren't killed—wounded."

"I shot low," yelled back Jack. "(Steer a little more to the west, there.) I shot low, and I don't think any got killed—though there's a lot of men that won't walk—and won't go plundering innocent rancheros—for a while.... Well, I had a good nap, and our little party back there has waked me up nicely. Better let me drive. I know this country fairly well."

Hike was glad to let him take the levers. Creeping back to the freight-platform, and covering himself with a fold of the tarpaulin against the piercing night-wind, he shivered off to sleep; worrying a little over the wounded men; hoping they were not killed; picturing the glorious excitement of a game on the athletic field at Santa Benicia, where they fought their best, but did not try to kill each other, to leave each other a mass of dead flesh on the field.

For the first time, Hike really understood that war is a horrible thing, to be prevented as far as possible. He remembered a friend of his father's, a brave, high-ranking officer and a good commander, who had often said that war was a crime, which the Army ought to prevent, instead of trying to bring it on. He was glad, as he lay there thinking, that he was with a man like Lieutenant Adeler, who also hated war, and who was coming down here not to make war, but to prevent the treacherous fighting of Welch. Welch was the sort of man who liked to bring about war.

He hoped that the tetrahedral, as used by the Army, would be so terrible a thing that it would prevent other nations from making war.

With the picture of the poor greasers, and a couple of Americans, writhing on the ground, mowed down by the machine-gun, bloody and in agonized pain, Hike prayed, simply and sincerely, for the end of all war.

He was not afraid. He was ready for the struggle about the ranch at Aguas Grandes. But he hoped that that struggle would end the warring of Welch.

He understood now something that Jack Adeler had said: that some day, before long, he hoped that the whole Army would be busy with great engineering, with building Panama canals, and stringing wires, and setting up wireless-stations, and making great forests, instead of preparing for fighting.

That, too, was what Hike wanted to do. He hoped, some day before long, to be an engineer, in good, stout laced leather boots and a sombrero, building a fine big steel bridge across some dangerous pass in the High Sierras, with the good open air and the deep woods about him. He planned to know wireless and aeroplanes and steel—and he hoped that every new thing he did, every fine bridge or aeroplane that he built, would be one step toward making a more civilized world, which would not want war; which would prefer happiness and peace and the good brave mountain woods to fighting like clay-grimed savages.

It was the first time that Hike really knew how serious he could be. He didn't feel much like a gay Santa Benicia boy, just then.

At last, exhausted, he fell asleep. He was awakened by the stopping of the motor, and, in the gray light of early dawn, saw that they were circling over a group of adobe buildings, with cattle corrals about, while a bunch of men were shouting, "He's here! Adeler's here!"

They were at Aguas Grandes.

CHAPTER XXIV

A SKIRMISH AT AGUAS GRANDES

"I DON'T trust that greaser that's guarding the south gate of the stockade," objected Hike.

"He? Why he's one of the safest men I've got," laughed Lieutenant Adeler.

They were making a tour of inspection, about the high fence of close-set barb-wire that had been built around the buildings of Adeler's ranch. They were dressed like cowpunchers, in furry chaps and sombreros.

"What about his having a brother who's with Welch?"

"Oh, I know about that, of course. Why, he's spoken to me of that brother a dozen times—sometimes with tears in his eyes."

"I wouldn't depend much on his tears," insisted Hike. "And last night I saw him talking to a fellow that was sneaking around outside the rancho, and that fellow looked so much like him that I'd bet anything that he was his brother."

"Oh, I can't believe he'd be treacherous," said Adeler. "He's been with me for nearly ten years, now. Besides, he knows which side his bread is buttered on. If he got kicked out of here, what could he do?"

"But I thought you said that most all of these greasers thought they'd be generals or presidents if the revolution succeeded, Lieutenant."

"Yes, but not Pedro. He's too wise, I'm certain."

For once, Hike disagreed with the Lieutenant, and determined to watch Pedro. That evening, when most of the men had gone to bed, Hike crept out and squatted in a corner by the lean-to grub-shanty, wrapped in a cloak. The moonlight made the desolate adobe building look like mounds of silver, and bunches of sage-brush like a fairy city. He could see Pedro, at the south gate, yawning and stretching; for he had been asleep all day, preparing for his night-watch. Hike watched quietly, but grew drowsier and drowsier.

Once, he thought he heard a noise near the machine-gun, which, with its cartridge-boxes, was mounted on a platform in the center of the ranch-yard. He even crept out of his nook, a little, keeping out of Pedro's sight. But there was no sign of any one near the gun, and, after this false alarm, he let himself drowse off more than ever.

He found himself springing bolt upright, staring at—what? He was still half asleep. Had he been having a nightmare? He patted his eyes with his finger-tips; then left his hand in the air, as though he had forgotten it there;

staring at the south gate. It was quietly swinging open, and through it slipped men in uniforms.

Instantly Hike yelled "Insurrectos! Insurrectos! Attack!"

There was a sound of shouting and alarm in the ranch houses, as Adeler's men woke up.

But the men creeping in at the gate were alarmed, too. Instantly they rushed into the ranch-yard, fully fifty of them, and toward the machine-gun. They climbed the platform, and loaded the gun into a cart.

In their midst Hike saw a man in uniform, with two revolvers. It was Willoughby Welch, once a real captain.

The insurrectos dashed toward the gate, with the gun, Hike ran after them, firing at Welch. He saw Welch rub his leg, as if winged, then swing about, still running, and fire.

A bullet clipped a lock of Hike's hair. He stopped, for a dozen insurrectos were facing about. Then, behind him, sounded Jack Adeler's voice, "Come on!" and the patter of a dozen men running.

At their head, Hike raced on, with Adeler. But by the time they reached the gate the insurrectos were off, on horseback, with the gun driven among them, in a fast light cart. Their shadows were already flashing along the moon-lit surface of the desert, among the thick gray patches of sage-brush and sparse grass.

With the Lieutenant, Hike rushed to the stables, and the men saddled at fever-heat. Not a word was heard, except "Where's my bridle?" "Tony, gimme some shells." The bunch all swung to saddle, and went galloping out of the ranch gate, slanting through it like a train on a curve, firing at the retreating insurrectos.

The Mexicans had stopped and formed about the cart, as a barricade. With rifles resting on the cart, they returned the fire. Tony Peries, at Hike's side, silently dropped off his horse. A party of twenty insurrectos darted out from their main bunch and circled.

"Back!" shrieked the Lieutenant. "Back, I tell you. We'll get surrounded. They're cutting us off."

"Aw—" came a yowl of protest from his men; but they turned and rode back to the ranch, as Adeler savagely shrieked "Back, I tell you," again.

Once inside the gate, they surrounded him, begging "Aw, let us at 'em."

"*No!*" snorted Jack. "I'm not leading any moving-picture-show charge. It'd be nice for all of us to get killed, 'cept that after that the insurrectos could do anything they wanted to. And they'd kill us, all right. They're fifty to fifteen. And they ain't fakers—they're Welch's Terrors—all of them horse-thieves or murderers, and all of them can ride. Ready now; they'll be shelling us with our own machine-gun. Or no—they didn't get the shells!

Hurray, we surprised them before they could take anything but the gun! Who gave that quick alarm? Whoever did—"

"It was Mr. Griffin," said the man who had been on guard at the east gate.

"Great! Hike," declared the Lieutenant. "You saved us from losing shells, and all—if it hadn't been for that alarm we'd be getting our own shells, right now."

"Please," said a greaser, "I shoot Pedro—he let in the insurrectos."

"All right—bury him to-morrow," said Adeler.

That was the end of the traitor.... Hike had seen him, cold and stiff, lying by the south gate, as they charged back into the ranch-yard. He felt that Pedro's death had been necessary, but it gave him a feeling of cold horror, just the same.... Pedro had been such a cheerful handsome Mexican, so much alive, waving his hands, laughing with dark, beautiful eyes, twisting his neat mustache, just a few hours earlier. He laid up that death not to Pedro but to Welch, and Welch's men, who had tempted Pedro; and he wanted to see this band of robbers ended, now and here.

"Lieutenant," he said, "let me fly over to Torreas in the *Hustle* and get another machine-gun. We can surprise the greasers with it, and end this."

"I wish you could, old Hike," mourned the Lieutenant, "but there's less than a quart of gasoline on the place. Barry is bringing some more, on a pack mule, and if he gets through the line of the insurrectos— Anyway, let's wait till to-morrow, and see what we can do."

Hike feared that Jack Adeler meant Barry was not very likely to get through; but he said nothing.

All that night, the ranch-yard was in a state of real siege. No one slept. They waited and watched, sheltered by the ranch-buildings. The moon was nearly down, and the light growing dimmer. At last it went down, and they had to patrol the fence.

Several times, little parties of the insurrectos rode up, fired through the barb-wire of the stockade, and tried to set buildings on fire. Jack Adeler's men, loving him and hating the robbers out there beyond the fence, were only too brave, rushing out to return the fire exposing themselves. One was killed, two were wounded. One of the worst of the bunch was Hike, till the Lieutenant threatened to imprison him if he didn't stay behind cover, firing from there.

"I didn't bring you down here to play melodrama hero," he snorted. "Anybody could *tell* that you're only a kid from the fool way you expose yourself. I brought you down here to help me run the *Hustle*, not to make grandstand-plays, and if you don't stay behind that wall—well, you see what you get. I won't even let you *see* the fun!"

Hike had to grin at Jack Adeler's pretending to be severe; but also he was afraid that the Lieutenant might keep his word, and imprison him in the house. After that, he stayed more under cover.

For two hours, there was a terrible time of waiting—waiting—every moment; peering out into the dark, wondering what the insurrectos were planning; holding themselves ready to drive back an attack. It was the hardest two hours of Hike's life, so far; to keep himself from sneaking out to the fence and joining the sentries patroling it.

Then came a yell at the fence, and he, with the others, dashed out a little and fired at the riders they could just make out in the before-dawn grayness. Then the ranch-yard was silent as the desert beyond.

With dawn, the insurrectos could be seen making off. This was Hike's chance to go for gasoline.

He said not a word to the Lieutenant. He was afraid that Adeler would not let him go. So he confided in his special friend and admirer, the man who had seen him give the alarm. Just at sunrise, he sneaked out of the east gate, on a fast pinto, bound for Anarcon and some gasoline for the *Hustle*.

Before the attack of the insurrectos, he had ridden about the place a good deal, with Jack Adeler, scouting for their enemies; and he knew both the country and his pinto well enough to be able to reach Anarcon. Also, he told himself, he was less needed for the actual defense of the ranch than the others. He could shoot well enough, but he hadn't the deadly aim of these men who had lived in a country where a quick pull of the gun means life.

He rode northward—straight away from the direction in which the insurrectos had gone; then curved over to eastward, heading for Anarcon.

Here he could find gasoline, for it was a station on the new automobile-road. To-day, in the desert, the automobile is becoming commoner and commoner. It permits the rancher to reach civilization, and the sheriff to reach savages! It may be found in desolate lands, in "the country that God forgot to finish," where one would expect nothing beyond cactus and the coyote.

As he rode, Hike tacked a little, watching for the enemies. He noticed a cloud of dust, finally, and cautiously rode toward it.

From a tiny butte, he saw a band of apparently about fifty, which he believed to be the men who had attacked them. They were just joining a larger band—not less than two hundred—who were riding southward. So Welch's Terrors were all together, then? There would not be much chance for the ranch to last long.

And Barry, who was expected with gasoline and other supplies, had gone clear off to Torreas, a good fifty miles away. Encumbered with the pack-mule, he could not possibly get back till night, Hike felt sure, even if he did escape the insurrectos.

It was up to him, Hike, then, to get back with gasoline, and be off with the tetrahedral, if he was to save the ranch from these two hundred and fifty robbers.

He rode as fast as he could kick his pinto into going, toward Anarcon, calmly taking a chance of the insurrectos catching sight of him. And, though they were a mile off, they *did* see him.

A couple followed him, firing at him as they got near, but he wasted no time in returning their fire, though his hand strayed longingly toward the revolver-belt draped across his chaps. He just pulled down the great brim of his sombrero, humped forward in the saddle, and rode as though they were already upon him.

The fast little pinto, too, heard the shots. That only made her go the faster. Also, she loved Hike, for Hike had ridden her these last four days, and he knew the combination of mastery and kindness which wins a horse.

At last the pursuers were left behind; and an hour later he rode into Anarcon.

Not till then did he remember that he hadn't a cent with him to pay for gasoline.

But he rode up to the absurd little shack labeled "GaRRagGe." At his shout, a lanky Texan came to the door, and looked at him suspiciously.

"Gasoline—quick—all you can load on this horse," he cried.

"Well, my boy, let's think about it," drawled the Texan. He looked as though he saw in Hike only a tall boy, the son of some rich Northerner ranching it in Mexico.

"Think about nothing," snorted Hike. "Insurrectos after our ranch. Got to have gasoline for aeroplane."

"Airyplane—boy, you're crazy," drawled the Texan again, maddeningly slow in speech. "Well, even if you *are*, you can have the gasoline if you pay for it."

"Adeler—he's got a ranch at Aguas Grandes—he'll pay for it."

"He'll pay for it right now, or he won't get it; not at this gara-jee," began the Texan, and stopped short, for Hike was looking at him across the sight of a leveled revolver.

The Texan threw up his hands and whined, "*All* right—just as you say, Mister. I guess Adeler is good for it."

He called his Mexican helper, and between them they loaded on the pinto as much gasoline, in cans, as she could carry. It was not much, but enough to take the *Hustle* to Torreas from Aguas Grandes. Twice, Hike saw the Texan's hand carelessly wandering toward a revolver, and each time he said "Look out," in a low and quiet voice, that meant business.

When the loading was finished, the Texan suddenly smiled. "I thought you was a boy," he stated, "but I take it back. You're crazy, all right—airy-

128

planes! But they grow nerve, where you come from. Where is that?"

"Hell," snapped Hike, "if I don't get back to it in time; but heaven if I do," and galloped off, leaving the Texan too astounded to take the pot-shot at Hike's back which he had planned.

With all this gasoline aboard, he had to ride back more slowly; keeping a look-out for the insurrectos. Twice he circled to avoid what looked like distant riders. He reached the ranch safely.

Jack Adeler himself rushed to open the east gate, shouting, "Where you been?"

"Gasolining," said Hike cheerfully, trying to look as grown-up as he could. "But that's nothing to where I'm going on the *Hustle*, right now."

"Oh, well," said Jack Adeler, resignedly, "I suppose there's no keeping you from getting killed.... Old man, I won't put it that way. If you've got the nerve to ride out and get gasoline, I'll just cut out the older brother air, and say 'Great work, old Hike.'"

He made Hike rest for an hour, and eat, incidentally, but an hour and seven minutes later, Hike rose from the ranch-yard in the *Hustle*, soared up to three thousand feet, and drove her toward Torreas at full speed.

CHAPTER XXV

THE RAIN OF DEATH

IT was fifty-seven and one half miles from the ranch at Aguas Grandes to Torreas, where a regiment of Mexican government or "federal" infantry, with a company of artillery, were encamped; and Hike made that distance, in the *Hustle*, in twenty-four and three quarters minutes, of which about seven minutes were spent in looking for the exact location of Torreas. So, less than half an hour after he had left the lonely ranch, he was astounding the soldiers by circling over their camp, and dropping in front of the commanding officer's headquarters.

Being a Mexican, the commander was excitable. He rushed out from his tent, and grasped Hike's hand, with immense respect and every show of honor, before Hike could say a word. Looking as dignified as possible, Hike delivered a note from Jack Adeler, asking for a machine-gun and a few soldiers.

The commandant scratched his beard a little, looked dubious, then glanced again at the marvelous complicated aeroplane, with Hike, straight and silent and dignified beside it. He nodded his head vigorously, and said, "*Madre de todos, si*—yesss, I do it!"

He sent two orderlies hurrying in different directions, while he poured on Hike a flood of questions in half English, half Spanish, about aeroplanes. While Hike was trying to answer, a squad of soldiers hurried up with a machine-gun and ammunition, which they loaded on the freight-platform. Directing them was a handsome, serious young lieutenant of infantry, introduced to Hike as Lieutenant Duros, who grasped Hike's hand with such awe and admiration that Hike had to warn himself not to get conceited. Suddenly he thought of two lines of the song of the Great Hazing:

> "And I have promised not to let my head get big again,
> When I go aviating on my airy aeroplane!"

and grinned a real Hike grin, which he hastened to turn into a smile of greeting to Lieutenant Duros.

"Can you ussss twelf soldiers?" asked the commander.

"Yes"—and twelve men were closely packed about the machine-gun, on the freight-platform, while Lieutenant Duros climbed into the front passenger-seat. Hike started the *Hustle* off easily. Except for a minute, at the yacht-wreck, he had never driven with anywhere near so many passengers.

130

But she took the load well. He shifted the speed-change lever to the third speed and they hummed through the air, while the soldiers yelled with surprise, and grabbed one another.

Through the motor-roar, Lieutenant Duros shouted a few sentences to Hike, treating him with such respect as one diplomat shows another. His English was excellent, though with a quaint little softening of the words.

"These revolutionists—they are not revolutionists," he cried. "We must wipe them out. I, I was with Madero, I was a *real* revolutionist. Me, I send many pesos the year to Russia, for the revolutionists there. I love freedom. But these men, they are robbers. We must wipe them out."

And so Hike suddenly remembered into what a terrible business of bloodshed they were plunging; but he shut his mouth grimly, and drove ahead, while Lieutenant Duros watched with admiration.

An hour and seven minutes after he had left the rancho, they swooped in sight of it. Surrounding the ranch were over two hundred insurrectos. They were attacking the gates with axes.

"Take 'em with the gun from the aeroplane," Hike howled to the Lieutenant, who saluted, crawled back to the machine-gun, and tried it. It was loaded.

Hike shut off the motor and volplaned down, directly over the thickest of the howling revolutionists. They fired a storm of bullets up at the *Hustle*, but Hike paid no attention to the bullets. He let her come down, slowly, and soared just over the heads of the insurrectos, who fled like frightened bronchos, bellowing with fear.

Lieutenant Duros aimed the machine-gun down, from the slowly sailing aeroplane. He let loose a shot a second, while the twelve soldiers fired in one continuous roaring stream. The revolutionists fell by dozens. Over their dead bodies stumbled fleeing wounded men.

Hike snapped on the motor, ascended to get leeway, and soared down again, over another bunch, on whom Lieutenant Duros let loose the machine-gun. He grimly kept her going thus, with the most delicate steering the tetrahedral had ever known; kept her just over the fleeing robbers.

One group made a stand, and Hike saw Captain Welch in the midst of it. "There's Welch—their leader—capture him—soldiers drop off!" he yelled to Lieutenant Duros, who saluted again, and shouted in rapid Spanish to his men.

They instantly dropped the fifteen feet to the ground, and as they did so Duros swept the group about Welch with the machine-gun. His supporters fell, a dozen men wounded and dying, and Welch himself clapped his hand to his side. Before he could recover, he was surrounded by federal soldiers, and hauled back toward the ranch.

Out from the ranch-yard came Jack Adeler's men, with Jack at the head, yelling and riding like demons. The Lieutenant swung from his horse, raised Welch, lifted him up and laid him across the saddle. Instantly he mounted, and rode back with the bleeding captive.

Three more circles were made with the tetrahedral. Sharpshooters in it picked out the fleeing insurrecto leaders, letting the privates escape. Lieutenant Duros, still smiling a fixed, hard, busy smile, once more turned the machine-gun loose—on a bunch of picketed horses of the insurrectos. Then he sat down, and held his head in his hands.

Hike brought the *Hustle* to earth, in front of the east gate.

"It was a glorious fight," Lieutenant Duros said, still hiding his head, as they landed. Then he lifted his head, and Hike was astounded to see that he looked very sick. "A glorious fight," he went on, "and it means the end of these robbers—but I am as sorry for every man I have to kill like he was my brother. *Santo Cuerpo!* Poor devils—they were just led by bad men." Then the Lieutenant straightened his shoulders, wiped his eyes, and climbed out of the *Hustle*, to greet Jack Adeler, who came charging down on them, shouting his thanks and admiration to Hike and the Mexican lieutenant.

"I know you are an American army officer," said Duros to Jack, "but do not be afeered, sir, for we shall keep it—uh—dark, is it? I congratulate you on the brilliant help you get from this other officer," motioning to Hike. "He is perhaps a lieutenant of the Signal Corps? I am still amaze to find him looking so young—I would think he is a—a—almost not a young man yet, if I have not seen him run the aeroplane."

"Me? An officer?" blushed Hike. "Why, I'm a kid—a youngster; that's all just a *muchacho*!"

The Mexican officer smiled at what he considered a jest and bowed, with his hand on his breast, "As you weesh, sir. You shall keep your disguise! With your permission—of course my commander have put me under your orders—I and my men, we will each take two of these horses of the insurrectos, and ride back to Torreas."

"Oh, let me take you back in the aeroplane," insisted Hike.

"The government needs the horses, permit me to say, sir?" He seemed to be begging for permission, still; and suddenly Hike realized with a shock that the Mexican officer *meant* it—that he, Hike, really had been and was commander of this expedition, and that Lieutenant Duros could do nothing without his permission!

"Very well, Lieutenant," he said, as gravely as he could. "You take command of the party, now, and take back all the horses you can handle. It's been a pleasure to meet you, sir, and permit me to congratulate you on the way you handled the machine-gun from the aeroplane. By the way, can you carry that on horseback?"

"Yes, sir, it is very light."

"Well, *adios, señor!*"

"Adios!" cried the Lieutenant, and gathered his men for the trek to Torreas.

When their backs were turned, Hike solemnly rolled over on the ground, and he was shouting with laughter when he arose. "Say, Jack, did you get that?" he howled to Adeler. "Me, a Santa Benician, a kid—and he thought I was an American Signal Corps officer. Say, wouldn't that *jar* you?"

For once Lieutenant Adeler did not see a joke. "Why," he said, quite seriously, "of course you do look awfully young, but from the way you handled the *Hustle*—and the federal troops—you might just as well be an officer, and a mighty good one. There were eighteen-year-old *colonels*, in the Civil War. And I know several men older than I who don't *look much* older than —"

"All *right*," said Hike. "Then just wait a minute till my wireless-man gets into communication with Washington, and I'll have General Thorne come down and black my shoes!"

"And now comes the worst part," sighed the Lieutenant, suddenly looking out over the desert. "We must bury the poor devils out there—must have been forty of them wiped out by that infernal machine-gun. Let's pray that we never fight except to bring peace, as we did here."

"Amen," said Hike, reverently.

CHAPTER XXVI

A KITE FOR WATCH-TOWER

"HIKE!" cried Lieutenant Adeler, suddenly. "There's a horrible possibility. Most of the revolutionists are going northwest—and the Widow Barston's rancho is off in that direction—they'd never notice it ordinarily, but they're sure to, the way they're going. Mighty few men on it—it's run by Mrs. Barston and her daughter."

"You think—they'd attack, just to get even?"

"I'm afraid so."

"Gee—we'll have to go help them," cried Hike. "I'm sorry we let Duros and his men go. How if I hurried after them, in the *Hustle*, and brought them back?"

Hike's suggestion didn't seem to lessen the anxiety of the Lieutenant, who sighed, "Nothing doing. Remember—they've got orders to report back to Torreas as soon as they can."

"Say, how if we—we two and maybe a couple of cowpunchers—went over to the Widow's ranch, in the *Hustle*, and hovered over it—just the sight of the machine would scare off any stragglers."

"Good idea—but, no, we haven't got much gasoline left."

"That's so," admitted Hike. "Not enough to hover for long. But SAY! Hover—hover—that gives me an idea. Get into the *Hustle*."

"What?"

"Yump. Come on. Will you? Would you mind? I've got a way to protect the Widow's ranch, and it won't take *any* gasoline, after we get there! We'll try the greatest experiment the *Hustle* has ever been put through!"

"All *right*!" laughed the Lieutenant.

Five minutes later, he was driving the tetrahedral toward the Widow's rancho.

"Please bring her down in the ranch-yard," directed Hike. The Lieutenant did so—wondering what this experiment was to be.

Hike explained. Martin Priest had told him, once, that the tetrahedral was the only aeroplane with so much stability that it could be used as a kite, a real kite. Anchored to the ground, with a long, heavy rope, it would probably float there, as long as the anchor held, float up there happily forever, without even an engine aboard.

But no one had ever quite dared to try it, before. It had to be tried now. They had to save the Widow Barston from the hungry, angry, straggling bands of rebels.

Out from the low, rough ranch-house, as they landed, came running a thin-faced, frightened woman, and her old maid daughter. Both were dressed in calico. They carried shotguns.

"Lieutenant Adeler—God bless you!" the mother shouted. "We were afraid the rebels were going to get us. Two have been sneaking around here."

"We'll watch for them. Have you some spare fence-wire?" asked Jack Adeler, quickly.

They stared in astonishment at such a question, but ran in and helped carry out several reels of wire.

Without saying a word, Hike and the Lieutenant began twisting this into a long, thin, strong rope, and binding one end to the gate-posts. The other end was hitched by a dozen small, twisted wires to the freight-platform of the *Hustle*, and immediately the machine plunged up into the air, with its steel "knife-string" glistening like silver as it uncoiled below them.

The fence-wire rope was three hundred feet long, but they shut off the motor at two hundred feet up. Instantly the *Hustle* floated along on the breeze, and came to a quiet halt when the anchor-rope drew tight.

Hike and Adeler held their breaths. Would the machine come tumbling down? Or would she become a kite? She did become a kite.

She floated up there, tugging at the rope, and swinging a little with each breath of wind, but safe and contented, shining in the sunlight.

"Bully, Hike, old man!" cried the Lieutenant. "You've given us our watch-tower."

From even two hundred feet up, they could see miles across the desert, and they watched for the rebel bands, through field glasses. Three times they saw dust-clouds in the distance, but each time the riders veered way off to the west as they made out the threatening tetrahedral poised in air.

When night came on, they camped—but not on the ground; no, indeed, not when they had a comfortable *Hustle* to sleep in! Coffee and flapjacks were made on the electrical stove, after running the engine for a few minutes to set the electric motor going, and then Hike crawled under a blanket, while the Lieutenant took the first turn watching.

So they hung at anchor till toward noon of the next day—two hundred feet up in the air. Then they left for the Lieutenant's rancho, got their things, and within an hour were whirling northward, bound for Santa Benicia.

* * * *

They were nearing Los Angeles, running easily and steadily at a hundred miles an hour, at dusk. The Lieutenant was driving.

Hike felt uneasy. The engine did not sound quite right. He could not make out quite what the trouble was, however.

Suddenly came a quick crash, from the engine. Hike knew that something had broken. Then the sound of back-fire, from a cylinder.

He dived from his seat, and slammed off the emergency-cock. Instantly, the flow of gasoline stopped, and the motor was dead.

He expected to have Jack Adeler ask "What did you shut off the cock for?" He didn't know just what he would answer.

But the Lieutenant merely planed down, circling till he could land in a patch of sand surrounding an orange-ranch.

As they stopped, the Lieutenant wiped his forehead, feverishly. Hike was astonished to see his face pale as a ghost's, in the twilight.

"Whew!" puffed Adeler. "Close call. Do you know what might have happened to us, if you hadn't shut off that emergency-cock just in time, Hike?"

"Why, no—but I thought there was some fire coming from one of the cylinders."

"There sure was. You know, on these motors with revolving cylinders, the exhaust-valve works automatically on a spring. Well, that spring broke. That let the fire spurt out—and it might have reached the fuel-tank. Know what might have happened then? Remember reading about several different aviators that got burned up, machines and all, up in the air? Well, fire reached their fuel tanks—that's all. If you hadn't jumped quick, every last plane might have been blazing, by now—and we burning alive, or blown to pieces. Hike, somehow, I'm glad you jumped quick!"

Hike didn't say a word. He merely sat down and imitated the Lieutenant, by wiping his forehead.

Then he got up, as if very tired—he really was a bit wobbly, yet, after thinking what they had escaped.

"I guess I'd better see if we can't get hold of a ranchero and a team, and get driven into the city, and have a spring sent out."

"Yes, go ahead," said the Lieutenant.

It was nearly noon, the next day, before he was able to send out a man with a repair-kit and assorted springs to the Lieutenant. Then he caught a train for San Francisco.

At last he was bound for the Academy again. For the first time since he had started for Mexico, he really remembered that he was a Sophomore at Santa Benicia, who might lose the glorious chance of playing in the San Dinero game because of his trip south.

In a few moments, he had become very much of a Santa Benician. The only question in the world was:

"Will they keep me out of the game? Will I be in decent trim to play, if they do put me in? Have my wind and nerve been hurt by the last few days?"

The fast train seemed scarcely to move, so anxious was Hike to get back, and see where he stood with the coach and Captain McDever.

CHAPTER XXVII

WILL HIKE PLAY?

HIKE got off the train at Santa Benicia, weary now and looking a little worn. It seemed strange to alight at this familiar dowdy wooden station, after the brilliant desert nights and the terrible grandeur of battle.

He walked slowly toward the Academy, and around a corner swung Bluggy Blodgett and two classmates, on a walk. "Hello, Hike," they cried excitedly. "Back?"

That same excited question as to whether he was back was asked by at least fifty before Hike reached Captain McDever's room, where he found McDever and the coach, talking over the coming afternoon's practise. They both rose from the window-seat, and, running him by the shoulders into a better light, by the windows, looked him over sharply. The coach shook his head. "You're pretty well done up. What you been doing?"

"Aeroplaning," was all Hike would say.

"Well, that may be all very well," said the coach severely, "but it doesn't put you into very good trim for football, strikes me. Now you beat it to your room, and I'll see that you get a good diet and rest, and there *may* still be a chance to put you in for the San Dinero game. But you can't play day after to-morrow—Saturday—Fresno game, at Fresno."

A week before the Thanksgiving game—a week during which he was treated as a baby. Hike protested, but he was overruled by a council of the coach, Bill McDever, and Poodle. He would have had the Lieutenant persuade them that he never did such good work as when he was tired. He thought of his ride to Anarcon and the battle, coming after a sleepless night of siege. But the Lieutenant had gone back to Mexico for a short time.

Hike had to submit to going to bed at eight-thirty, and to eating nothing more exciting than beefsteak and oatmeal. He had to avoid all "nervousness"—by which the coach meant hard practise, horseback riding, fierce boxing, and everything else that was interesting. In their place, he had foolish bendings and twistings, nice easy exercises which bored him excessively.

Though Hike was fairly obedient, the coach's gloom did not get less. Hike had, one evening, the sudden terrible thought that he really and truly might not be allowed to play.

There was another danger, as well. Hike's Latin was the poorest of his studies, and on the Monday before the game (which came on Thursday),

"Old Grouch," the Latin and Greek teacher, was going to have an important test for the Sophomores. A flunk in it would disqualify from playing.

Poodle took him in charge, in Latin—at which the cheerful poet was a shark. Every evening, just when Hike was planning a new sort of elevating plane or rotary valve, spoiling perfectly good pieces of paper with criss-cross lines, Poodle would slam the table three times, to get attention, open a grammar of Latin, or the travels of Julius Cæsar (who was so good at Latin that he wrote in it), and then make poor Hike listen to rules, which he pronounced idiotic, or battles of Cæsar, which Hike called, "prett' slow fighting."

"Well, maybe you think I like doing this better'n you do," Poodle would protest, whereupon Hike would get very sorry and fairly good and have some more Latin poured into him.

As a result, he passed the test. But, at the last moment, would the coach think that he was "rested up" enough to be in condition to play?

Though the coach had been a good player himself, he was something of a crank. He seemed to believe that the best way to make a bunch of eleven men feel like Sandows was to find out what each of them most wanted to do, and then prevent each from doing it.

Hike was willing to cut out the pie, though he had a sneaking fondness for it. He was willing—that is, nearly willing—to go to bed at eight-thirty. But when it came to having to "rest" all the time, he felt like going on a strike, by himself, and throwing bricks at Captain McDever and the coach. The less they let him plunge into hard practise, the less fit he felt.

Tuesday, two days before the game, was a horrible day. He felt so depressed that he scarcely cheered up at a telegram from General Thorne, announcing that P. J. Jolls and his thugs had been sentenced to long terms in the Federal Penitentiary.

On the Wednesday evening before the game, Hike finally decided he had "rested" so much that he simply wouldn't be able to play.

"You really might be better if you snook out and took a ride, or something," Poodle mused, as they sulked, in their room.

"Poodle, you're a genius. No wonder the school mag. took both your poems! Sure—that's what I need—and that's what I'll get! Jump into your puttees and riding-breeches, and come on!"

"But Hike—" protested Poodle.

Hike drove him to the closet, and began stripping off both their clothes, all at once, laughing and singing, "We stung 'em, see!"

Though most of what the livery stable keeper called "the young gentlemen from the Academy" wanted nice, easy-going horses, these two demanded the two fierce, half-broken bronchos that the stableman called "Fiend" and "Demon."

By now, once they had thus broken the coach's rules, Poodle was as interested as Hike, and he hummed blithely as they flung a leg over the rearing bronchos, and rode out into the rain.

Rain? Rather! California was making up for her usual dry summers by laying in a supply of the wettest water in the clouds. It poured till they could scarcely see the street lamps, and the mud splashed over them at every plunging step the bronchos took.

At first, Hike was a little uncomfortable, after his lazy week; but as they raced down the hill, with the wet wind full in his face, the mud spurting about him in the darkness, he stood in his stirrups and whooped, and kicked "Fiend" into a crazy lope about equal to an express train's. His cheeks glowed, his legs felt strong enough for anything as his thighs gripped the horse's sides.

They took five miles, at a good pace. Then Hike regretfully drew up and shouted back to Poodle (who had been jarred almost to death): "Well, I suppose we can't go much farther."

"Yes-s-s-s," shivered Poodle, horribly aware that there was a large river down the back of his neck. "I think this is enough exercise. 'Course I'd like to take back all the mud there is on my pants, but I'm afraid I'd get smothered, and Bluggy owes me thirty cents and I want to live and make him pay it."

"Right O!" said Hike. "But just one more spurt," and he set "Fiend" off at the lope again; swinging around a curve, leaning far out from the saddle and swinging his hat gayly, glad to feel the cold rain on his bare head.

Then he rode back to Poodle and shouted, "I feel great, now. This's something *like* training! Watch me play to-morrow. I'll eat the San Dinero gentlemen."

Poodle was cold and gloomy and pessimistic, by this time.

"I hope you do," he said, as though he didn't believe it.

"So do I, Pood'. Look here. I s'pose I'm a fool but—if San Dinero licks us—I'll wish I'd never seen an aeroplane, or Mexico. Gee, I wish the game were on, right now."

They were a little quiet as they loped back to the stable.

CHAPTER XXVIII

THE BIG GAME

THE Santa Benicia team came on the field, after the first half, with Left Eared Dongan in the line-up. Pink Eye Morrison had hurt his ankle, at left end, and had been replaced by Dongan. Otherwise, they had gone through the first half without injury, and the score was six to six.

Was Hike in the game? Rather. When the coach saw him on Thursday morning, bright of eye and ruddy of cheek, there was no question of his going in. "What did you do to get in such good shape?" he asked.

"Rested *right*," replied Hike.

He had never played so well, though he did not try for any spectacular runs. He was making sure that Santa Benicia, rather than Hike Griffin, should win.

The teams held each other down well, during the second half, and then Hike got around the San Dinero end with the ball. He had practically a clear field before him. The Santa Benicians were ready to spring up and yell their "hike, Hike, *hike!*"

But on his shoulder Hike felt the touch of Left Ear's hand. Left Ear had followed him, close and swift, as interference. There was a kind of thrill in this support from Poodle's old enemy. Left Ear could make the touch-down, with this clear field and—

Hike suddenly passed him the ball and yelled, "*Beat it!*" Dazed, Left Ear seized the ball and ran faster than he had ever run before. He was winded when he dropped on San Dinero's goal-line, but he had made the touch-down that won the game.

A few minutes more of playing, and the Santa Benicians flocked on the field, yelling "Victory!" and carried off Pink Eye, Bill McDever, Left Ear and Hike on their shoulders—though Poodle still declares that it was Hike who got most of the cheers.

What Hike cared for more was the hand-shake of three people: Left Ear, who looked curious about the eyes as he said, "Thanks, old Hike"; Poodle; and—Lieutenant Jack Adeler!

"Just got back in time for the game," the Lieutenant said. "The country's been pacified, and the robber bands broken up. But there's one piece of bad news. Captain Welch got free, and he's disappeared again."

"Got *free*?!"

"Yes. Through a corrupt judge. He must have done some tall bribery. He got a writ of habeas corpus, and the judge declared that there were no grounds for holding him. Not even under bail. Then he made a quick disappearance. I have no idea where he's gone; but I don't think he's very likely to love us any too well, and he'll make more trouble for us, yet. We must watch out for him."

"We sure will."

* * * *

While they were talking, and walking up to the Lieutenant's room with Poodle, Left Eared Dongan was gathering the class for a special meeting. The regular class-meeting to elect a president had been postponed till after the Thanksgiving game. Mousey Tincom and others had insisted on the postponement, fearing that Bluggy Blodgett, the class bully, might get the office. Hike and Poodle did not know that there was a meeting.

Left Eared Dongan had been expected to nominate Bluggy Blodgett. He jumped to his feet before Mousey Tincom could, rushed up to the blackboard facing the class-room where the meeting was held, and shouted, "I nominate the best man in the class."

Then, with a large flourish, he wrote: "Hike G."

"I move to make that unanimous," shouted Biffer Townsend, and half the class yelled "Second t' motion." It was carried, with even Bluggy Blodgett yelling with the rest.

When Hike and Poodle left the Lieutenant's room, they were met by most of the class, on their way to the bonfire to celebrate the San Dinero victory. As they marched, they sang to the tune of "Son of a Gambolier," a new song which Left Eared Dongan had written on the blackboard:

> "Oh, you can have most any foolish president you like,
> But we're a brainy bunch of Sophs., and we have chosen *Hike*!
> Just watch our speed—it's us that's aviating down the pike,
> Get wise, be still, and listen to our '*hike*, Hike, hike!'"

That night the team met, and elected Snifty Carter, from the Junior class, for the next year's captain. Snifty met Hike after the great bonfire, late in the evening, and said, "Hike, I hope you'll be on the job footballing, next year."

"I sure will," promised Hike.

"Because," added Snifty, "the whole school will expect you to win the game for us."

"Aw—" was all Hike could say, in astonished protest.

But he looked forward to a great spring, with the track-team, and a great fall to come.

A LETTER FROM POODLE

"A. READER, ESQ.:

"Some think I ought to be in on the end of this, too, but I don't care so awfully much just so Hike has all the credit that is coming to him! But I might say that I think I'll land anyway one poem a month from now on, and maybe some stories, in the school mag.

"It's a January evening, and old Hike is studying hard, in his Morris chair, on the other side of the fireplace from where I'm writing. He's been hitting the books hard, and I guess he'll make up that Latin.

"I think there will be some fun next spring. Besides the track team, probably we will be organizing a Santa Benicia band of Boy Scouts, and even though Hike and I do feel so awful grown up, watch us connect with all the fun.

"Lieutenant Jack Adeler is organizing the band, and he has a plan to take the scouts on a long outing next summer, down the coast below Monterey.

"I think we'll have an exciting time, for I've heard that there's a bunch of Chinese smugglers down there, in caves and so on, and horse thieves.

"So when you're getting ready for scouting, remember that Hike and I send you a wireless 'Hullo.' Maybe we can even lend you some leggins or frying pans by wireless. Good luck, anyway.

"Well, I'm kind of sleepy, and there's a fine young bed waiting for me, and

"So long!

"Poodle Darby."

THE END

www.ingramcontent.com/pod-product-compliance
Lightning Source LLC
Chambersburg PA
CBHW011448170626
46816CB00008B/2569

* 9 7 8 1 4 7 9 4 9 9 8 1 6 *